KOLYMA TALES

KOLYMA TALES

BY *Varlam Shalamov*

TRANSLATED FROM THE RUSSIAN
BY JOHN GLAD

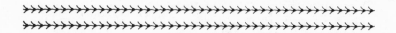

W·W·NORTON & COMPANY·NEW YORK·LONDON

W. W. Norton & Company, Inc., 500 Fifth Avenue, New York, N. Y. 10036
W. W. Norton & Company, Ltd., 25 New Street Square, London EC4A 3JA

✔✔✔✔✔ *The text of this book is composed in photocomposition Primer. Display type is Monotype Deepdene. Composition and manufacturing are by the Maple-Vail Book Manufacturing Group. Book design is by Marjorie J. Flock.*

Library of Congress Cataloging in Publication Data
Shalamov, Varlam Tikhonovich.
  Kolyma Tales.
  Translation of Kolymskie rasskazy.
  I. John Glad. II. Title
PZ4.S52697Ko 1980 [PG3487.A592] 891.7'3'42 79-20245

ISBN 0-393-01324-3

 3 4 5 6 7 8 9 0

Contents

>>

Foreword   7

Part One ⚔ SURVIVAL

A "Pushover" Job   21
In the Night   26
Shock Therapy   29
In the Bathhouse   39
Carpenters   46

Part Two ⚔ HOPE

Dry Rations   55
Sententious   70

Part Three ⚔ DEFIANCE

Prosthetic Appliances   79
Quiet   81
Major Pugachov's Last Battle   89

Part Four ⚔ THE CRIMINAL WORLD

On Tick   107
A Piece of Meat   112
The Snake Charmer   121

Part Five ⚔ THE JAILORS' WORLD

Chief of Political Control   131
A Child's Drawings   135
The Injector   138
Magic   140
My First Tooth   144
The Lawyers' Plot   151

Part Six ⚘ THE AMERICAN CONNECTION

Lend-Lease   173
Condensed Milk   181

Part Seven ⚘ RELEASE

Esperanto   189
The Train   196
The Used-Book Dealer   206

Foreword

>>>

KOLYMA TALES are stories of the Soviet forced-labor camps located in the Kolyma (kah-lee-*mah*) region of northeastern Siberia. The well-known historian Robert Conquest, in his study of the area, estimates that three million people met their deaths there. As an absolute minimum, he sets the figure of two to two and one-half million. His estimates are based on ships' records, accounts of firsthand witnesses, and other reliable, although necessarily incomplete, sources.

It might seem incredible that the closest estimate the Western scholar can produce is "give or take a million," but one must remember that historians have no direct access to the records, that there has been no Nuremberg Trial complete with captured archives, witnesses, and so forth. Shalamov, in the tremendously powerful story "Lend-Lease," writes of having learned of an enormous mass grave:

> With my exhausted, tormented mind I tried to understand: How did there come to be such an enormous grave in this area? I am an old resident of Kolyma, and there had been no gold mined here as far as I knew. But then I realized that I knew only a fragment of the world surrounded by a barbed-wire zone and guard towers that reminded one of the pages of tent-like Moscow architecture. . . . I realized that I knew only a small bit of that world, a pitifully small part, that twenty kilometers away there might be a shack for geological explorers looking for uranium or a gold mine with thirty thousand prisoners. Much can be hidden in the folds of the mountain.
>
> And then I remembered the greedy blaze of the fireweed, the furious blossoming of the taiga in summer when it tried to conceal in the grass and foliage any deed of man—good or bad. And if I forget, the grass will forget. . . .

Varlam Shalamov, a man with an enormous literary talent and an incredibly tragic life, has not forgotten. The stories and sketches given here do not attempt to provide a statistical analysis of the fates of the millions murdered in Kolyma. Rather, they are a vivid account of individual moments in the lives of individual men, for only in the particular can we begin to comprehend the horror of the whole. Even so, it is impossible to appreciate the enormity of this tragedy. Were there two and one-half or were there three million victims? We can never come to grips emotionally with a statistic of that sort, any more than we can appreciate that one star is a hundred million light years from us and another a hundred fifty million.

By his own admission, Solzhenitsyn barely touches on the Kolyma region in *The Gulag Archipelago*. He writes that when he first came upon an anthology of Shalamov's poetry, he "trembled as if he were meeting a brother." He asked Shalamov to co-author *The Gulag Archipelago* with him, but Shalamov—already an old, sick man—declined. Nevertheless, Solzhenitsyn writes: "Shalamov's experience in the camps was longer and more bitter than my own, and I respectfully confess that to him and not me was it given to touch those depths of bestiality and despair toward which life in the camps dragged us all."

Kolyma is an enormous area with the coldest temperatures in the Northern Hemisphere. The area is so desolate and isolated that in 1927 there were only 7,580 inhabitants in an area five or six times the size of France! In 1932–33 foundations were laid for a massive forced-labor area intended to produce gold for the young Soviet state.

The years 1937–39 were the years of the purges. Millions of people were arrested, held for months in appalling prison conditions, tried under ridiculous charges, and either executed or sent in cattle cars to Siberia. Emaciated from hopelessly inadequate diet, denied even sufficient drinking water and toilet facilities, freezing from the cold, they would arrive at the Siberian ports of Vladivostok, Vanino, or Nakhodka after a trip that lasted anywhere from thirty to forty days! There they were held in concentration camps for varying periods of time and sent by ship to Kolyma. Michael Solomon, a Rumanian who had been a prisoner in the camps, described the experience:

When we came out on to the immense field outside the camp I witnessed a spectacle that would have done justice to a Cecil B. DeMille production. As far as the eye could see there were columns of prisoners marching in one direction or another like armies on a battlefield. A huge detachment of security officers, soldiers and signal corpsmen with field telephone and motor-cycles kept in touch with headquarters, arranging the smooth flow of these human rivers. I asked what this giant operation was meant to be. The reply was that each time a transport was sent off, the administration reshuffled the occupants of every cage in camp so that everyone had to be removed with his bundle of rags on his shoulder to the big field and from there directed to his new destination. Only 5,000 were supposed to leave, but 100,000 were part of the scene before us. One could see endless columns of women, of cripples, of old men and even teenagers, all in military formation five in a row, going through the huge field, and directed by whistles or flags.[1]

Conditions on the ships were appalling. Solomon describes the hold of a ship carrying women:

We climbed down a very steep, slippery wooden stairway with great difficulty and finally reached the bottom. It took us some time to accustom our eyes to the dim light of the dingy lower deck.

As I began to see where we were, my eyes beheld a scene which neither Goya nor Gustave Doré could ever have imagined. In that immense, cavernous, murky hold were crammed more than 2000 women. From the floor to the ceiling as in a gigantic poultry farm, they were cooped up in open cages, five of them in each nine-foot-square space. The floor was covered with more women. Because of the heat and humidity most of them were only scantily dressed; some had even stripped down to nothing. The lack of washing facilities and the relentless heat had covered their bodies with ugly red spots, boils, and blisters. The majority were suffering from some form of skin disease or other, apart from stomach ailments and dysentery.

At the bottom of the stairway we had just climbed down stood a giant cask, on the edges of which, in full view of the soldiers standing on guard above, women were perched like birds, and in the most in-

1. Michael Solomon, *Magadan* (Toronto: Vertex, 1971), p. 82.

credible positions. There was no shame, no prudery, as they crouched there to urinate or to empty their bowels. One had the impression that they were some half-human, half-bird creatures which belonged to a different world and a different age. Yet, seeing a man coming down the stairs, although a mere prisoner like themselves, many of them began to smile and some even tried to comb their hair. Who were these women? And where had they come from? I asked myself. I soon learned that they had been arrested all over Russia and those countries of Europe overrun by Soviet armies. The main accusation against them was collaboration with the enemy.[2]

Although there was some lead mining, fur trapping, and a fishing industry in Kolyma, the chief occupation of the prisoners was gold mining. At least at first. After a time, gold production was very nearly subordinated to the task of extermination. Because of the geography of the region—its isolation and the mountains cutting off the only path out by land— there was no real opportunity for escape. It was no secret that people were brought to Kolyma to die and produce some gold in the process. The world described in these stories leaves little room for any other conclusion. Hitler once remarked that he had learned a great deal from the Soviets—not so much in the area of ideology as in methodology.

The attitude of the West toward this state of affairs has been truly amazing. Ships such as the one already described were purchased from England, Holland, and Sweden. In the summer of 1944, Professor Owen Lattimore, representing the Office of War Information, and Henry Wallace, vice-president of the United States, visited Kolyma and wrote glowing accounts of it. Lattimore said the Soviet effort "could roughly be compared to a combination of the Hudson Bay Co. and T.V.A."[3]

The other side of the coin, of course, has been the violently anti-Western propaganda practiced in the Soviet press for more than sixty years. In the "corrective labor camps" the official position was most direct. After the original Communist

2. Ibid., p. 85.
3. *National Geographic*, December 1944, p. 657.

defeats during the Korean conflict, there were rumors that the Americans would try to take Kolyma. One prisoner reports being told that plans had been made in the event of an Allied landing: "We shall blow up the mine entrances and you will die like rats, 200 yards below ground without seeing a single American or British uniform."[4]

Shalamov's stories are in the Chekovian tradition: a brief plot devoted to one incident (although occasionally less compact than Chekov's); an objective dispassionate narration intended to provide a contrast to the horror of the moment; and a *pointe* at the end.

The affinities with Chekov's work are not confined to structure. Savelev's monologue in "Dry Rations" could have been taken from a Chekov play:

Just imagine. . . . We'll survive, leave for the mainland, and quickly become sick old men. We'll have heart pains and rheumatism, and all the sleepless nights, the hunger, and long hard work of our youth will leave their mark on us even if we remain alive. We'll be sick without knowing why, groan and drag ourselves from one dispensary to another. This unbearable work will leave us with wounds that can't be healed, and all our later years will lead to lives of physical and psychological pain. And that pain will be endless and assume many different forms. But even among those terrible future days there will be good ones when we'll be almost healthy and we won't think about our sufferings. And the number of those days will be exactly equal to the number of days each of us has been able to loaf in camp.

The narrator in Shalamov's stories is an unusually passive one. He is always the victim, and almost never initiates action of his own. Rarely does he speak. His hopes and plans extend no further than a few hours: to getting warm, to receiving an extra piece of bread. He is capable of admiring men of action. Major Pugachov, who leads an escape attempt in "Major Pugachov's Last Battle," is lionized, but this path of action remains a fantasy for the author himself. Even so, Pugachov ends his life by committing suicide.

Shalamov, the narrator and participant in these stories, is

4. Solomon, *Magadan*, p. 119.

always watching, observing. In the story "Train" he and a young man play a game, guessing the age and professions of their fellow passengers. In the story "Magic," two men select people for specific jobs in the camps. Those to be selected are equally filthy and ragged and appear quite uniform in their misery. Nevertheless, the two men determine the former professions of the convicts and make their selection solely by appearance, and are usually correct.

As one reads these stories, the feeling of horror is mixed with amazement that Kolyma could have occurred in our enlightened age and that the victims permitted it to happen. As in the camps of Fascist Germany, one could say that people had the option of suicide, if not resistance. Shalamov responds:

I believed a person could consider himself a human being as long as he felt totally prepared to kill himself, to interfere in his own biography. It was this awareness that provided the will to live.

I checked myself—frequently—and felt I had the strength to die, and thus remained alive.

Much later I realized that I had simply built myself a harbor, avoided the question, for at the critical moment I would not be the same man as I am now when the question of life or death would be an exercise of the will. I would inevitably weaken, become a traitor, betray myself. Instead of thinking of death, I simply felt that my former decision needed some other answer, that my promises to myself, the oaths of youth, were naïve and very artificial.[5]

Shalamov's biography is largely contained in these stories. He was born in 1907 and first began to publish in 1932. In 1937 he was arrested in one of the great "purges" for the crime of having declared the Nobel Prize laureate, Ivan Bunin, a classic author of Russian literature. Shalamov writes that he spent nearly seventeen years in the camps, so he must have been released sometime in 1954.

5. Varlam Shalamov, "Zhizn' inzhenyera Kipreeva" [The life of engineer Kipreev], in idem, Kolymskie rasskazy [Kolyma tales] (London: Overseas Publications Interchange, 1978), p. 734 (translated by John Glad; the story is not included in this English edition).

At present, only Shalamov's poetry can be published in the USSR, and reviewers are forced to write nonsense such as: "He [Shalamov] writes primarily about nature. One gets the impression that his surroundings interest him only on an impressionistic level."

Occasionally, however, clues are provided for the careful reader. In one review of Shalamov's work, the well-known writer Boris Slutsky quotes a conversation Slutsky once had with the poet Zabolotsky. Zabolotsky pointed to a house under construction and mentioned that he had been a laborer, a mason, a carpenter, and a building foreman in his day. The remark, seemingly irrelevant in a review of a collection of verse, immediately tips off the reader to Shalamov's fate. Zabolotsky was himself a prisoner in the camps—a fact well known to educated Russians. Thus, the reader realizes that Shalamov is one of those who survived the camps.

With time, it has become evident to the Soviet government that Shalamov's prose writings cannot be ignored. Aside from their artistic merit, they are of major documentary significance. "The Used-Book Dealer," for example, reveals that the state first began to experiment with the misuse of psychiatry and chemical will suppressants as early as the late 1930s in the infamous Zinoviev, Pyatakov, and Bukharin show trials in 1938.

Shalamov's stories were first circulated in manuscript form within the USSR, and were later published in Russian in the emigré journals *The New Review* and *Grani*. A complete Russian-language edition of his work was published in London in 1978 by Overseas Publications Interchange. In France three different editions of his work have appeared and editions are being prepared for publication in other languages. All carry a similar publisher's note: "The following stories appear without the knowledge or consent of the author and he should not be held responsible for their publication."

The Soviet government has been placed in an embarrassing situation: Shalamov could have been prosecuted and his writings branded with the usual "slander of Soviet reality." That, however, would have drawn attention to him. Western newspapers are largely interested in writers who have already attracted public attention. On numerous occasions the Soviet government has proved to be its own worst enemy by reattacking its victims and thus serving as press agent for the authors under attack. If one considers the so-called dissident authors, one is struck by the fact that many are actually apolitical and owe their press coverage to absurd government persecution. Pasternak, Akhmatova, Zoshchenko, and Brodsky might serve as examples. In the case of the politically oriented writers, the government has radically damaged its image by becoming a defender of its own Stalinist heritage.

In the case of Shalamov, it was evident that his stories were a major document of our time and any attempt to discredit them would only increase interest in them.

To appreciate the position of the Soviet government, one must understand that the USSR is in reality the former Russian Empire passing itself off as one country. Although Western newspapers often refer to the Soviet Union as "Russia," Russian is only one among one hundred thirty languages spoken in this empire which occupies one-sixth of the world's inhabited land mass. Moreover, in a few years Russians will no longer constitute a majority within the country. One does not need to be a historian to recall what has happened to other empires. Gone are Austro-Hungary and the Ottoman Empire. France, England, Spain, and Portugal have long since divested themselves of their colonies. The curious paradox is that the Russian Empire, renamed and christened with a new ideology, continued to expand up until the mid-1940s, under the banner of decolonialization. It even succeeded in encircling itself with satellites in Eastern Europe and Asia, not to mention other true believers scattered over the globe. Considering that China alone has a population of one billion, that was no small accomplishment. Now, however, China has challenged the "sacred and inviolable" Soviet borders and even declared war with the USSR to be a virtual inevitability. The satellites' former unflinching loyalty grows less and less reliable, and within the USSR itself, nationalistic, religious, and ethnic groups—while on the surface relatively docile—are threatening in their sheer numbers.

The chroniclers of our times, the Shalamovs and the Solzhenitsyns, have drawn a picture of the methodology which held this enormous empire together. The secret was mass terror in which not only outright opponents of the regime were liquidated, but also potential opponents (and their families and friends). Not only were executioners executed, but the same fate befell the executioners of the executioners of the executioners. Such was the glue of terror binding this enormous structure.

Since Stalin's death, however, all this has changed. Savage terror has been replaced by a heavy-handed bureaucracy of mind-boggling dimensions. The burning question of our age is: Can the empire be maintained without the former glue? The Soviet leaders possess an enormous advantage never dreamed of by former emperors, kaisers, and tsars: their subjects are not merely citizens required to follow the law of the land, they are "company men," direct employees of the state which is the sole owner of the means of production. Newspapers and books no longer pass through the censor— they are written by the censor. Can this degree of control hold the empire together until it metamorphoses into a country in which the speakers of a hundred thirty languages are reborn as "Soviet citizens"? That is the question that troubles the men in the Kremlin. No bureaucracy has ever dismantled itself in the past, and the Soviet leaders feel the enormous stirrings that can lead to war and revolution.

It is against this background that men like Shalamov appear. The greater their talent, the greater the danger they represent. The regime is faced with the dilemma of either renouncing its own heritage of terror or eliminating the embarrassing witnesses. The "cult of personality" has indeed been renounced—but in a guarded fashion. As for embarrassing witnesses, a number of solutions have been tried, ranging from reimprisonment to exile. These approaches, however, have often simply provided an additional embarrassment in that the regime appears once more to be espousing Stalinism. Shalamov's case is unusual in that he was forced merely to sign a short statement to the effect that "the thematics of his work were no longer topical." The authorities now hold their breath, hoping his work will pass unnoticed in the flood of testimony of other victims. This more subtle approach has proved effective in dealing with a sensation-oriented Western press, but Shalamov is too major a writer to be ignored. His time has come, and he himself has described his "moment of truth":

Maxmutov struck the tree trunk with a geologist's hammer and the tree resonated in a dull echo, the sound of a hollow trunk, of emptiness, of life. A weasel, a tiny beast, fell directly onto the path. The beast did not disappear in the grass, the taiga, the forest. Its eyes gleaming with despair and fearlessness, the weasel looked up at the men. She was about to give birth and her contractions continued right there in front of us on the path. Before I managed to do anything, to shout, to comprehend, to stop him, the geologist shot the weasel point-blank with his small-caliber rifle. There was always the possibility of encountering a bear, and the rifle was loaded with a piece of lead. Maxmutov was a bad shot. . . .

The wounded weasel crawled along the bear path directly at Maxmutov, and he backed up, retreating before her gaze. The hind leg of the pregnant weasel had been shot completely off, and she dragged behind her a bloody cereal of tiny, unborn beasts—the young she would have borne an hour later when Maxmutov and I would have been far from the broken fir and which would have gone out into the difficult forest world of wild animals.

The weasel crawled toward Maxmutov, and I could read courage, anger, vengeance, and despair in her eyes.[6]

This book contains only a selection of Shalamov's stories. I have translated those which I literally felt compelled to see appear, but I have been struck by the lack of unanimity on the

6. Idem, "Khrabrye glaza" [Brave eyes], in ibid, pp. 411–412 (translated by John Glad; the story is not included in this English edition).

part of other readers as to which are the most powerful. Certainly, such a selection necessarily involves an element of arbitrariness, and I sincerely hope that the complete stories will eventually appear in English.

———

Special thanks are due to Susan Ashe, Norman di Giovanni, Diana Glad, Ellery McClintock, and Larisa Romanov for their generous and talented assistance in the preparation of this book.

John Glad

College Park, Maryland
May 1979

PART ONE

SURVIVAL

A "Pushover" Job

>>

THE HILLS glistened white with a tinge of blue—like loaves of
sugar. Round and bare of forest, they were smothered with a
layer of dense snow compacted by the winds. In the ravines
the snow was deep and firm; a man could stand on it. But on
the slopes it swelled up in enormous blisters. These were
shrubs of Siberian dwarf cedar which lay flat on the ground to
hibernate through the winter—even before the first snow fell.
They were what we had come for.

Of all northern trees, I loved the dwarf cedar most of all.

I had long since come to understand and appreciate the
enviable haste with which poor northern nature shared its
meagre wealth with equally indigent man, blossoming for him
with every variety of flower. There were times when everything bloomed in a single week and when only a month after
the beginning of summer the almost never-setting sun would
make the mountains flame red with cowberries and then
darken with their deep blue. Rowan shrubs hung heavy with
full, watery berries—so low you didn't even have to raise your
hand. Only the petals of the mountain sweetbrier smelled like
flowers here. All the others exuded a sense of dampness, a
swampy odor, and this seemed appropriate to the spring silence, both of the birds and the larch forest whose branches
slowly clothed themselves in green needles. The sweetbrier
clung to its fruit right into winter and from under the snow
stretched out to us its wrinkled, meaty berries whose thick vio-
let skin concealed a dark-yellow flesh. I knew of the playful
vines which again and again changed their color in spring
from dark rose to orange to pale green, as if they were
stretched with dyed kidskin. The slender fingers of the larch

with their green fingernails seemed to grope everywhere, and
the omnipresent, oily fireweed carpeted the scenes of former
forest blazes. All this was exquisite, trusting, boisterous,
rushed; but all this was in summer when dull green grass
mixed with the glaze of mossy boulders that gleamed in the
sun and seemed not gray or brown, but green.

In winter it all disappeared, covered with crusty snow cast
into the ravines by the winds and beaten down so hard that to
climb upward a man had to hack steps in the snow with an ax.
Everything was so naked that a person in the forest could be
seen half a mile away. And only one tree was always green,
always alive—the dwarf cedar. The tree was a weatherman.
Two or three days before the first snow in the cloudless heat of
fall when no one wanted even to think of the oncoming winter,
the dwarf cedar would suddenly stretch out its enormous five-
yard paws on the ground, lightly bend its straight, black, two-
fist-thick trunk, and lie prone on the earth. A day or two would
pass and a cloud would appear; toward evening a snowstorm
would begin. And if in the late fall low gray snow clouds would
gather accompanied by a cold wind and the dwarf cedar did
not lie down, one could be sure that no snow would fall.

Toward the end of March or in April, when there was still
no trace of spring and the air was dry and rarified as in winter,
the dwarf cedar would suddenly rise up, shaking the snow
from its reddish-green clothing. In a day or two the wind
would shift, and warm streams of air would usher in spring.

The dwarf cedar was a very precise instrument, sensitive
to the point where it sometimes deceived itself, rising during a
lengthy period of thaw. But it would hurriedly lie back in the
snow before the cold returned. Sometimes we would make a
hot campfire in the morning to last till evening so we could
warm our hands and feet. We would heap on as many logs as
possible and set off to work. In two or three hours the dwarf
cedar would stretch its branches out from under the snow and
slowly right itself, thinking that spring had arrived. But before
the fire could even go out, the tree would again lie back into

the snow. Winter here is two-toned: a high pale-blue sky and the white ground. Spring would lay bare the dirty yellow rags of fall, and the earth would be clothed in this beggar's garb for a long time—until the new greenery would gather its strength and begin to blossom furiously. In the midst of this pitiless winter and gloomy spring, the dwarf cedar would gleam blindingly green and clear. Moreover, tiny cedar nuts grew on it, and this delicacy was shared by people, birds, bears, squirrels, and chipmunks.

Having selected an area of the hill shielded from the wind, we dragged a considerable number of small and large branches into a heap and gathered some dry grass where the wind had bared the mountain. We had brought several smoking logs with us from the barracks stove; there were no matches here.

We carried the logs in a large tin can with a wire handle attached, and had to be careful that they didn't go out along the way. Removing the charred logs from the can, we blew on them and set the smouldering ends together. I kept blowing until they began to burn and then I set them on the dry grass and twigs. All this we covered with larger branches, and soon an uncertain tail of blue smoke trailed downwind.

I had never before worked in gangs that gathered dwarf cedar needles. We did everything by hand, plucking the green, dry needles and stuffing them into sacks; in the evening we handed them over to the foreman. The needles were hauled away to a mysterious "vitamin factory" where they were boiled down into a dark-yellow viscous extract with an inexpressibly repulsive taste. Before each dinner this extract had to be drunk or eaten—however a person could manage. Its taste spoiled not only dinner, but supper as well, and many considered this "treatment" a supplementary means of camp discipline. But without a shot glass of this medicine it was impossible to get dinner in the cafeteria; the rule was strictly enforced. Scurvy was everywhere and dwarf cedar was the only medically approved cure. It was ultimately proved that this

preparation was completely ineffective in the cure of scurvy
and the "vitamin factory" was closed. Nevertheless, faith con-
quers all, and at the time many drank the stinking abomina-
tion, went away spitting, but eventually recovered from
scurvy. Or they didn't recover. Or they didn't drink it and
recovered anyway. Everywhere were enormous clumps of
sweetbrier, but no one prepared it or used it against scurvy
since the instructions from Moscow said nothing about sweetbrier. (A few years later sweetbrier was brought in from the
"mainland," but it was never prepared locally.)

The instructions prescribed cedar needles as the only
source of vitamin C. On that day I was assigned to gather the
precious raw material. I had gotten so weak that I was transferred from the gold mine to needle picking.

"I'll put you on dwarf cedar for a while," the job assigner
told me in the morning. "It'll be a pushover job for a few days."

"Needle picking" was considered not just an easy job, but
the easiest of all. Moreover, it didn't require the presence of a
guard.

After many months of work in the icy mines where every
sparklingly frozen stone burned the hands, after the clicks of
rifle bolts, the barking of dogs, the swearing of the overseers
behind our backs, needle gathering was an enormous pleasure, physically felt with every exhausted muscle. Needle
gatherers were sent out after the others, while it was still dark.

It was a marvelous feeling to warm your hand against the
can with the smouldering logs and slowly set out for the seemingly unattainable peaks, to climb higher and higher, constantly aware of your own solitariness and the deep winter
silence of the mountains. It was as if everything evil in the
world had been snuffed out and only you and your companion
existed on this narrow, dark, endless path in the snow, leading
upward into the mountains.

My companion watched my slow motions disapprovingly.
He had been gathering cedar needles for a long time and correctly surmised in me a weak, clumsy partner. Work was done

in pairs, and the "wage" was a joint one, divided fifty/fifty.

"I'll chop and you pick," he said. "And get a move on, or we won't fill our quota. I don't want to have to go back to the mines."

He chopped down a few branches and dragged an enormous pile of green paws to the fire. I broke off the smaller branches and, starting with the top of each branch, pulled off the needles together with the bark. They looked like green fringe.

"You'll have to work faster," said my companion, returning with a new armload.

I could see that the work was not going well, but I couldn't work faster. There was a ringing in my ears, and my fingers, frostbitten at the beginning of winter, ached with a familiar dull pain. I yanked at the needles, broke entire branches into smaller pieces without stripping the bark, and stuffed the product into the sack. The sack wouldn't fill. Before the fire rose a mountain of stripped branches that looked like washed bones, but the sack kept swelling and swelling and accepting new armfuls of needles.

My companion sat down next to me, and the work went faster.

"It's time to go," he said suddenly. "Or else we'll miss supper. We haven't got enough here for the quota." He took from the ashes of the fire a large stone and shoved it into the sack.

"They don't untie them there," he said frowning. "Now we've met our quota."

I stood up, scattered the burning branches, and kicked snow onto the red coals. The fire hissed and went out, and it immediately became cold. It was clear that evening was close. My companion helped me heave the sack onto my back. I staggered under its weight.

"Try dragging it," my companion said. "After all, we're going downhill, not up."

We barely arrived in time to get our soup. No meat or vegetables were given for such light work.

In the Night

>>>

SUPPER WAS OVER. Slowly Glebov licked the bowl and brushed the bread crumbs methodically from the table into his left palm. Without swallowing, he felt each miniature fragment of bread in his mouth coated greedily with a thick layer of saliva. Glebov couldn't have said whether it tasted good or not. Taste was an entirely different thing, not worthy to be compared with this passionate sensation that made all else recede into oblivion. Glebov was in no hurry to swallow; the bread itself melted in his mouth and quickly vanished.

Bagretsov's cavernous, gleaming eyes stared into Glebov's mouth without interruption. None of them had enough will power to take his eyes from food disappearing in another's mouth. Glebov swallowed his saliva, and Bagretsov immediately shifted his gaze to the horizon—to the large orange moon crawling out onto the sky.

"It's time," said Bagretsov. Slowly they set out along a path leading to a large rock and climbed up onto a small terrace encircling the hill. Although the sun had just set, cold had already settled into the rocks that in the daytime burned the soles of feet that were bare inside the rubber galoshes. Glebov buttoned his quilted jacket. Walking provided no warmth.

"Is it much farther?" he asked in a whisper.

"Some way," Bagretsov answered quietly.

They sat down to rest. They had nothing to say or even think of—everything was clear and simple. In a flat area at the end of the terrace were mounds of stone dug from the ground and drying moss that had been ripped from its bed.

"I could have handled this myself," Bagretsov smiled

wryly. "But it's more cheerful work if there are two of us. Then, too, I figured you were an old friend . . ."

They had both been brought on the same ship the previous year.

Bagretsov stopped: "Get down or they'll see us."

They lay down and began to toss the stones to the side. None of the rocks was too big for two men to lift since the people who had heaped them up that morning were no stronger than Glebov.

Bagretsov swore quietly. He had cut his finger and the blood was flowing. He sprinkled sand on the wound, ripped a piece of wadding from his jacket, and pressed it against the cut, but the blood wouldn't stop.

"Poor coagulation," Glebov said indifferently.

"Are you a doctor?" asked Bagretsov, sucking the wound.

Glebov remained silent. The time when he had been a doctor seemed very far away. Had it ever existed? Too often the world beyond the mountains and seas seemed unreal, like something out of a dream. Real were the minute, the hour, the day—from reveille to the end of work. He never guessed further, nor did he have the strength to guess. Nor did anyone else.

He didn't know the past of the people who surrounded him and didn't want to know. But then, if tomorrow Bagretsov were to declare himself a doctor of philosphy or a marshal of aviation, Glebov would believe him without a second thought. Had he himself really been a doctor? Not only the habit of judgment was lost, but even the habit of observation. Glebov watched Bagretsov suck the blood from his finger but said nothing. The circumstance slid across his consciousness, but he couldn't find or even seek within himself the will to answer. The consciousness that remained to him—the consciousness that was perhaps no longer human—had too few facets and was now directed toward one goal only, that of removing the stones as quickly as possible.

"Is it deep?" Glebov asked when they stopped to rest.

"How can it be deep?" Bagretsov replied.

And Glebov realized his question was absurd, that of course the hole couldn't be deep.

"Here he is," Bagretsov said. He reached out to touch a human toe. The big toe peered out from under the rocks and was perfectly visible in the moonlight. The toe was different from Glebov's and Bagretsov's toes—but not in that it was life-less and stiff; there was very little difference in this regard. The nail of the dead toe was clipped, and the toe itself was fuller and softer than Glebov's. They quickly tossed aside the remaining stones heaped over the body.

"He's a young one," Bagretsov said.

Together the two of them dragged the corpse from the grave.

"He's so big and healthy," Glebov said, panting.

"If he weren't so fattened up," Bagretsov said, "they would have buried him the way they bury us, and there would have been no reason for us to come here today."

They straightened out the corpse and pulled off the shirt.

"You know, the shorts are like new," Bagretsov said with satisfaction.

Glebov hid the underwear under his jacket.

"Better to wear it," Bagretsov said.

"No, I don't want to," Glebov muttered.

They put the corpse back in the grave and heaped it over with rocks.

The blue light of the rising moon fell on the rocks and the scant forest of the taiga, revealing each projecting rock, each tree in a peculiar fashion, different from the way they looked by day. Everything seemed real but different than in the day-time. It was as if the world had a second face, a nocturnal face.

The dead man's underwear was warm under Glebov's jacket and no longer seemed alien.

"I need a smoke," Glebov said in a dreamlike fashion.

"Tomorrow you'll get your smoke."

Bagretsov smiled. Tomorrow they would sell the un-derwear, trade it for bread, maybe even get some tobacco. . . .

Shock Therapy

>>>

DURING ONE blissful period in his life Merzlakov had worked as a stable hand and used a homemade huller—a large tin can with a perforated bottom—to turn oats intended for the horses into human food. When boiled, the bitter mixture could satisfy hunger. Large workhorses from the mainland were given twice as much oats as the stocky, shaggy Yakut horses, although all the horses were worked an equally small amount of time. Enough oats were dumped in the trough of the monstrous Percheron, Thunder, to feed five Yakut horses. This was the practice everywhere, and it struck Merzlakov as being only fair. What he could not understand was the camp's rationing system for people. The mysterious charts of proteins, fats, vitamins, and calories intended for the convicts' table did not take a person's weight into consideration. If human beings were to be equated with livestock, then one ought to be more consistent and not hold to some arithmetical average invented by the office. This terrible "mean" benefited only the lightweight convicts who, in fact, survived longer than the others. The enormous Merzlakov—a sort of human analogue to the Percheron, Thunder—felt only a greater gnawing hunger from the three spoons of porridge given out for breakfast. A member of a work gang had no way of supplementing his food supply, and furthermore, all the most important foodstuffs —butter, sugar, meat—never made it to the camp kettle in the quantities provided for by the instructions.

Merzlakov watched the larger men die first—whether or not they were accustomed to heavy labor. A scrawny intellectual lasted longer than some country giant, even when the latter had formerly been a manual laborer, if the two were fed on an equal basis in accordance with the camp ration. Not calculated for large men, the basic nourishment could not be essentially improved even by food bonuses for heightened productivity. To eat better, one had to work better. But to work better one had to eat better. Estonians, Latvians, and Lithuanians were always the first to die—a phenomenon that the doctors always explained away by claiming that peoples of the Baltic states were weaker than Russians. True, their normal way of life was more dissimilar to that of the camps than was the world of the Russian peasant, and it was more difficult for them. The primary reason, however, was quite different: it wasn't that they possessed less endurance, but that they were physically bigger than the Russians.

About a year and a half earlier, Merzlakov had arrived as a newcomer at the camp. In a state of collapse from scurvy, he had been allowed to work as a stand-in orderly in the local clinic. There he learned that medical dosages were determined according to the patient's weight. New medicines were tested on rabbits, mice, or guinea pigs, and human dosages were then calculated according to body weight. Children's dosages were smaller than adult dosages.

The camp food ration, however, had no relation to the weight of the human body, and it was precisely this improperly resolved question that amazed and disturbed Merzlakov. But before he completely lost his strength, he miraculously managed to get a job as a stable hand so he could steal oats from the horses to stuff his own stomach. Merzlakov was already counting on surviving the winter. Perhaps something new would turn up in the spring. But it didn't work out that way. The stable manager was fired for drunkenness and the senior groom—one of those who had taught Merzlakov how to make a huller—took his place. The senior groom had himself stolen no small amount of oats in his day, and he knew exactly how it was done. Wanting to impress the administration and no longer in need of oatmeal for himself, he personally smashed all the hullers. The stable hands began to fry or boil oats and eat them unhulled, no longer making any distinction between their own stomachs and that of a horse. The new manager reported this, and several stable hands, including Merzlakov, were put in solitary for stealing oats. From there they were dismissed from the stable and returned to their former jobs—in the general work gang.

In the general work gang Merzlakov soon realized that death was near. He staggered under the weight of the logs he had to carry. The foreman, who had taken a dislike to this husky man, forced Merzlakov to carry the thick end of the log every time. At one point Merzlakov fell and, unable to get up from the snow, in a moment of decision refused to carry the damn log any farther. It was already late and dark. The guards were hurrying to their political indoctrination session; the workers wanted to return to the barracks, to food; and the foreman was late for a battle at cards. Merzlakov was the cause of the entire delay, and he was punished. At first his comrades beat him, then the foreman beat him, then the guards. The log remained lying in the snow; instead of the log, they carried in Merzlakov. He was freed from work and lay on his berth. His back ached. The paramedic rubbed it with machine grease since there were no rubbing compounds in the first-aid room.

Merzlakov kept waiting, half bent over and insistently complaining of pains in the small of the back. The pain had long since disappeared, the broken rib quickly healed, and Merzlakov was attempting at any price to save himself from being signed out to go back to work. And they didn't sign him out. At one point they dressed him, put him on a stretcher, loaded him into the back of a truck, and transferred him together with some other patients to the regional hospital. There was no X-ray machine there, and it was time to think things over seriously. Merzlakov did precisely that. For several months he lay bent in two and was finally transferred to a central hospital which, of course, had an X-ray machine and where Merzlakov was placed in the surgical division. In the traumotological ward the patients in their simplicity referred to the ward as the "dramatological" ward, not even realizing the bitterness of the pun.

"This one," said the surgeon, pointing to Merzlakov's chart, "we're transferring to you, Peter Ivanovich. There's nothing we can do for him in surgery."

"But you write in your diagnosis—'ankylosis resulting from a trauma of the spine.' What am I supposed to do with him?" asked the neuropathologist.

"Well, yes, ankylosis, of course. What else can I write? After beatings, even worse things turn up. I remember there was an incident at the Sery Mine. The foreman beat one of the men. . . ."

"I haven't got time to listen to your incidents, Seryozha. I ask you, why are you transferring him to me?"

"It's all written down. He has to be examined before we can make up the papers. You poke him with needles for a while, we do the papers, and we put him on the boat. Let him be a free man."

"But you did X-rays? You should be able to see any problems without needles."

"We did X-rays. Take a look." The surgeon held the dark film negative up to a gauze curtain. "The devil himself couldn't find anything in that picture. And that kind of smear is all your X-ray technicians will ever produce until we get regular current."

"What a mess," said Peter Ivanovich. "Okay, let's let it go at that." And he signed his name to the history of the illness, giving his consent to transfer Merzlakov to his own ward.

The surgical ward was noisy and confusing. The northern mines were serious business, and the ward was filled with cases of frostbite, sprains, broken bones, burns. Some of the patients lay on the ward floor and in the corridors where one totally exhausted young surgeon with four assistants could only manage three or four hours of sleep a day and had no time to examine Merzlakov carefully. Merzlakov knew that the real investigation would begin in the neuropathological ward.

His entire despairing convict will was concentrated on one thing: not to straighten out. And he did not straighten out, much as he wanted to—even for a moment. He remembered the gold mine; the cold that left him breathless with pain; the frozen, slippery stones, shiny with frost; the soup he slurped without any spoon; the rifle butts of the guards and the boots of the foremen. And he found within himself the strength not to straighten out. Already it was easier than it had been the first few weeks. Afraid to straighten out in his sleep, he slept little, knowing that all the attendants had orders to keep an eye on him and unmask his duplicity. And after such an unmasking he would be sent to a "penal mine." What must such a penal mine be like, if even an ordinary one left Merzlakov with such terrible memories?

On the day after his transfer, Merzlakov was taken to the doctor. The head doctor asked briefly about the origin of the illness and shook his head in sympathy. He remarked in passing that even healthy muscles forced into an unnatural position for many months could become accustomed to the position and a man could make himself an invalid. Then Peter Ivanovich took over the examination. Merzlakov responded at random to needle pricks, pressures, and taps with a rubber hammer.

Peter Ivanovich spent more than half of his time exposing fakers. He, of course, understood the reasons for their conduct. Peter Ivanovich had himself recently been a prisoner, and he was not surprised by the childish stubbornness of the fakers or the primitiveness of their tricks. Peter Ivanovich, a former associate professor at a Siberian medical institute, had laid his own scientific career to rest in those same snows in which the convicts were saving their lives by deceiving him. It was not that he lacked pity for people, but he was more of a doctor than a human being; first and foremost he was a specialist. He was proud that a year of hard labor had not beaten

the doctor, the specialist out of him. He understood his task of
exposing cheaters—not from any lofty, socio-governmental
point of view and not from the viewpoint of morality. Rather,
he saw in this activity a worthy application of his knowledge,
his psychological ability to set traps, into which hungry, half-
insane people were to fall for the greater glory of science. In
this battle of doctor and faker, the doctor had all the advantages—thousands of clever drugs, hundreds of textbooks, a
wealth of equipment, aid from the guards, and the enormous
experience of a specialist. The patient could count only on his
own horror before that world from which he had come and to
which he feared to return. It was precisely this horror that lent
him the strength for the struggle. In exposing any faker, Peter
Ivanovich experienced a deep satisfaction. He regarded it as
testimony from life that he was a good doctor who had not yet
lost his qualifications but, on the contrary, had sharpened
them, who could still "do it."

"These surgeons are fools," he thought, lighting up a cigarette after Merzlakov had left. "They either don't know or
have forgotten topographic anatomy, and they never did know
reflexes. They get along with X-rays alone, and without X-rays
they can't even diagnose a simple fracture. And the bullshit
they throw around!" It was crystal clear to Peter Ivanovich
that Merzlakov was a faker. "Let him stay for a week. We'll get
all the tests worked up to make sure the formalities have been
observed and glue all those scraps of paper into the history of
the illness." Peter Ivanovich smiled in anticipation of the theatrical effect of the new exposé. In a week a new group of patients would be shipped back to the mainland. The reports
were compiled right here in the ward, and the chairman of the
board of medical commissioners would arrive to examine personally the patients prepared by the hospital for departure. His
role amounted to examining the documents and checking that
the formalities had been observed; an individual examination
of the patient took thirty seconds.

"My lists," said the surgeon, "contain a certain Merzlakov. The guards broke his back a year ago. I want to send him

home. He was recently transferred to Neuropathology. The papers for his departure are ready."

The chairman of the commission turned to the neuropathologist.

"Bring in Merzlakov," said Peter Ivanovich.

The bent-over Merzlakov was led in; the chairman glanced at him.

"What a gorilla," he said. "But I guess there's no reason to keep that kind around." Pen in hand, he reached for the lists.

"I won't give my signature," said Peter Ivanovich in a clear, loud voice. "He's a faker, and tomorrow I will have the honor to prove that to both you and the surgeon."

"Let's set him aside then," said the chairman indifferently, putting his pen down. "And, in general, let's wrap things up. It's already getting late."

"He's a faker, Seryozha," said Peter Ivanovich, taking the surgeon by the arm as they were leaving the ward.

The surgeon withdrew his arm.

"Maybe," he said with a disgusted frown. "Good luck in exposing him. I hope you get your kicks out of it."

The next day Peter Ivanovich gave a detailed report on Merzlakov to the head of the hospital at a meeting.

"I think," he said in conclusion, "we'll expose Merzlakov in two stages. The first will be the Rausch narcosis that you forgot, Seryozha." Triumphantly, he turned to the surgeon. "That should have been done right away. And if the Rausch doesn't produce any results, then . . ." Peter Ivanovich spread his hands in a gesture of resignation. "Then we'll have to try shock therapy. I assure you, that can be very interesting."

"Isn't that going too far?" Alexandra Sergeevna asked. She was a heavy woman who had recently arrived from the mainland. Here she ran the tubercular ward—the largest ward in the hospital.

"Not for that son of a bitch," the head of the hospital answered.

"Let's wait and see what kind of results we get from the Rausch," Peter Ivanovich inserted in a conciliatory fashion.

Rausch narcosis consisted of a stunning dose of ether for a short-term effect. The patient would be knocked out for fifteen or twenty minutes, giving the surgeon time to set a dislocation, amputate a finger, or open a painful abscess.

The hospital bigwigs, dressed in white gowns, surrounded the operating table at the dressing station where the obedient, stooped-over Merzlakov was brought. The attendants reached for the cotton strips normally used to tie patients to the operating table.

"No, no," shouted Peter Ivanovich. "That's totally unnecessary."

Merzlakov's face turned upward, and the surgeon placed the anesthetic mask over it, holding a bottle of either in his other hand.

"Let's begin, Seryozha!"

The ether began to drip.

"Deeper, breathe deeper, Merzlakov. Count out loud."

"Twenty-six, twenty-seven," Merzlakov counted in a lazy voice, and, suddenly breaking off his count, started to mutter something fragmented, incomprehensible, and sprinkled with obscenities.

Peter Ivanovich held in his hand the left hand of Merzlakov. In a few minutes the hand fell limp. Peter Ivanovich dropped it, and the hand fell softly onto the edge of the table, as if dead. Peter Ivanovich slowly and triumphantly straightened out the body of Merzlakov. Everyone gasped with amazement.

"Now tie him down," said Peter Ivanovich to the attendants.

Merzlakov opened his eyes and saw the hairy fist of the hospital director.

"You slime," he hissed. "Now you'll get a new trial."

"Good going, Peter Ivanovich, good going!" the chairman of the commission kept repeating, all the while slapping the neuropathologist on the shoulder. "And to think that just yesterday I was going to let him go!"

"Untie him," Peter Ivanovich commanded. "Get down from that table."

Still not completely aware of his surroundings, Merzlakov felt a throbbing in his temples and the sickeningly sweet taste of ether in his mouth. He still didn't understand if he was asleep or awake, but perhaps he had frequently had such dreams in the past.

"To hell with all of you!" he shouted unexpectedly and bent over as before. Broad-shouldered, bony, almost touching the floor with his long, meaty fingers, Merlakov really looked like a gorilla as he left the dressing station. The orderlies reported to Peter Ivanovich that patient Merzlakov was lying on his bed in his usual pose. The doctor ordered him to be brought to his office.

"You've been exposed, Merzlakov," the neuropathologist said. "But I put in a good word for you to the head of the hospital. You won't be retried or sent to a penal mine. You'll just have to check out of the hospital and return to your previous mine—to your old job. You're a real hero, brother. Made us look like idiots for a whole year."

"I don't know what you're talking about," the gorilla said without raising his eyes from the floor.

"What do you mean, you don't know? We just straightened you out!"

"Nobody straightened me out."

"Okay, friend," the neuropathologist said. "Have it your own way. I wanted to help you out. Just wait. In a week you'll be begging to check out."

"Who knows what'll happen in a week," Merzlakov said quietly. How could he explain to the doctor that an extra week, an extra day, even an extra hour spent somewhere other than the mine was his concept of happiness. If the doctor couldn't understand that himself, how could he explain it to him? Merzlakov stared silently at the floor.

Merzlakov was led away, Peter Ivanovich went to talk to the head of the hospital.

"We can handle this tomorrow, and not next week," the head of the hospital said upon hearing Peter Ivanovich's suggestion.

"No, I promised him a week," Peter Ivanovich said. "The hospital won't collapse."

"Okay," the head of the hospital said. "We can handle it next week. But be sure to send for me when you do. Will you tie him down?"

"We can't," the neuropathologist said. "He could dislocate an arm or a leg. He'll have to be held down." Merzlakov's case history in his hand, the neuropathologist wrote "shock therapy" in the treatment column and inserted the date.

Shock therapy consisted of an injection of camphor oil directly into the patient's bloodstream. The dose was several times that used in hypodermic injections for seriously ill coronary patients. It produced a sudden seizure similar to seizures of violent insanity or epilepsy. The effect of the camphor was a radical heightening of muscle activity and motor ability. Muscle strain was increased incredibly, and the strength of the unconscious patient was ten times that of normal.

Several days passed, and Merzlakov had no intention of voluntarily straightening out. The morning of the date scheduled in the case history arrived, and Merzlakov was brought to Peter Ivanovich. In the north any sort of amusement is treasured, and the doctor's office was packed. Eight husky orderlies were lined up along the wall. In the middle of the office was a couch.

"We'll do it right here," Peter Ivanovich said, getting up from behind the desk. "No sense going to surgical ward. By the way, where is Sergei Fedorovich?"

"He can't come," Anna Ivanovna, the physician on duty, said. "He said he was busy."

"Busy, busy," Peter Ivanovich repeated. "He ought to be here to see how I do his job for him."

The surgeon's assistant rolled up Merzlakov's sleeve and smeared iodine on Merzlakov's arm. Holding the syringe in his right hand, the assistant inserted the needle into a vein next to the elbow. Dark blood spurted from the needle into the syringe. With a soft movement of the thumb the assistant depressed the plunger, and the yellow solution began to enter the vein.

"Pump it in all at once," Peter Ivanovich said, "and stand back right away. You," he said to the orderlies, "hold him down."

Merzlakov's enormous body shuddered and began to thrash about even as the orderlies took hold of him. He wheezed, struggled, kicked, but the orderlies held him firmly and he slowly began to calm down.

"A tiger, you could hold a tiger that way," Peter Ivanovich shouted in near ecstasy. "That's the way they catch tigers in the Zabaikal region." He turned to the head of the hospital. "Do you remember the end of Gogol's novel, *Taras Bulba*? 'Thirty men held his arms and legs.' This gorilla is bigger than Bulba, and just eight men can handle him."

"Right," the head of the hospital said. He didn't remember the Gogol passage, but he definitely enjoyed seeing the shock therapy.

While making rounds the next morning Peter Ivanovich stopped at Merzlakov's bed.

"Well," he said. "What's your decision?"

"I'm ready to check out," Merzlakov answered.

In the Bathhouse

>>

IN THOSE cutting jokes that are unique to the camps, the bathhouse sessions are often referred to as tyranny. A traditional ironic formula originating within the camp's very obser-

vant criminal element runs: "Tyranny! The politicals are being
herded into the bathhouse." This joking remark is fraught
with bitter truth.

The bathhouse is a negative event, a burden in the convict's life. This observation is a testimony of that "shift of values" which is the main quality that the camp instills in its inmates.

How can that be? Avoidance of the bathhouse constantly
perplexes both doctors and camp officials who view this ab-
senteeism as a kind of protest, a violation of discipline, a sort of
challenge to the camp regime. But fact is fact and the bathhouse ritual, practiced over the years, represents an event in
the life of the camp. The guards are mobilized and instructed,
and all the supervisors, not to mention the guards, personally
take part in catching truants. Running the bathhouse and
disinfecting clothes in the steam rooms is the direct and official responsibility of the Sanitation Squad. The entire lower
administrative hierarchy consisting of convicts (group leaders,
foremen) also abandons its normal affairs and devotes itself to
the bathhouse. Ultimately even production supervisors are
inevitably drawn into this great event. An entire gamut of
production measures are applied on bathhouse days (three a
month).

On these days everyone is on his feet from early morning
to late at night.

How can this be? Is it possible that a human being, no
matter what state of deprivation he might be reduced to, will
refuse to wash himself in the bathhouse and free himself from
the dirt and sweat that cover his body with its festering skin
diseases? Can it be that anyone would refuse to feel cleaner, if
only for an hour?

There is a Russian phrase: a person may be referred to as
"happy as if he just came from the bathhouse." Indeed, the
phrase accurately reflects the physical bliss experienced by a
person who has just washed himself.

Can it be that people have so lost their minds that they do

not understand, do not want to understand, that life is better without lice than with them? There are a lot of lice in the crowded barracks and they can't be eliminated without the disinfestation chamber.

Of course, infestation is a relative concept. A dozen or so lice in one's clothing doesn't count. Infestation begins to trouble both the doctors and one's comrades when the lice can be brushed off one's clothing, when a wool sweater stirs all by itself through flea power.

Thus, can it be that a human being—no matter who—would not want to free himself from this torment that keeps him from sleeping and against which he struggles by scratching his own dirty body till it bleeds?

No, of course not. But the first "but" arises over the lack of any work-release time for the bathhouse. Bathhouse sessions are arranged either before or after work. After many hours of work in the cold (and it's no easier in the summer) when all thoughts and hopes are concentrated on the desire to reach one's bunk and food so as to fall asleep as soon as possible, the bathhouse delay is almost unendurable. The bathhouse is always located an appreciable distance from living quarters, since it serves not only convicts but civilians from the village as well. Usually it is situated in the civilian village, and not in camp.

The bathhouse always takes up much more than the hour necessary to wash and delouse clothing. Many people have to wash themselves, one group after the other, and all latecomers have to wait their turn in the cold. They are brought to the bathhouse directly from work without any stopover in camp, since they would all scatter and find some way to evade going there. When it's very cold the camp administration attempts to shorten the outside waiting period and admits the convicts directly to the dressing rooms. The dressing rooms are intended for ten to fifteen persons but the camp authorities pack in up to a hundred men in outer clothing. The dressing rooms are either unheated or poorly heated. Everything and everyone is mixed together—naked men and men in coats. There is a constant shoving, swearing, and general hubbub. Profiting from the noise and the crush, both common criminals and political prisoners steal their neighbors' belongings. Different work gangs who live separately have been brought together, and it's never possible to recover anything. Furthermore, there's nowhere to entrust anything for safekeeping.

The second, or rather, the third "but" arises from the fact that the janitors are obliged to clean up the barracks while the work gang is in the bathhouse. The barracks are swept, washed, and everything judged to be unnecessary is mercilessly thrown out. In camp every rag is treasured, and enormous amounts of energy are expended to acquire a spare pair of mittens or extra foot rags. Bulkier things are treasured even more, and food highest of all. All this disappears without a trace and in full accordance with the law while the convicts are in the bathhouse. It's useless to take things to work with you and from there to the bathhouse; they are immediately noticed by the vigilant and experienced eye of the camp criminal element. Mittens or foot rags can be easily exchanged for a smoke.

It is characteristic of man, be he beggar or Nobel laureate, that he quickly acquires petty things. In any move (having nothing to do with jail) we are amazed at the number of small things we have accumulated and cannot imagine where they all come from. And all these possessions are given away, sold, thrown out—until we achieve with great difficulty the level necessary to close the lid of the suitcase. The same is true of the convict. He is, after all, a working man and needs a needle and material for patches, and an extra bowl perhaps. All this is cast out and then reaccumulated after each bathhouse day, unless it is buried somewhere deep in the snow to be dug up again the next day.

In Dostoevsky's time the bathhouse provided one basin of hot water (anything over that had to be paid for). That standard has been retained to this very day. It's always a wooden basin with not very hot water. Prisoners are permitted any amount of those burning pieces of ice that stick to the fingers; they're kept in barrels. There's never a second basin to dilute the water, and the hot water is cooled by the pieces of ice. That, however, is all the water a convict receives to wash the hair on his head and his entire body.

A convict must be able to wash himself with any portion of water—from a spoonful to a cistern full. If he gets only a spoonful, he wets his gummy festering eyes and considers his toilet completed. If he gets a cistern of water, he splashes it on his neighbors, refills his basin every minute, and somehow manages to use up his portion in the allotted time.

All this testifies to quick-wittedness in the resolution of such an everyday question as the bathhouse. But it does not, of course, solve the question of cleanliness. The dream of getting clean in the bathhouse is an impossible dream.

In the bathhouse itself there is constant uproar accompanied by smoke, crowding, and shouting; there's even a common turn of speech: "to shout as in the bathhouse." There is no extra water, and no one can buy any. But it's not just water that's in short supply. There's not enough heat either. The iron stoves are not always red-hot the way they should be, and most of the time it's simply cold in the bathhouse. The feeling of coldness is increased by a thousand drafts from under the doors, from cracks. Cracks between the logs are stuffed with moss which quickly dries up and turns to powder, leaving holes to the outside. Every stay in the bathhouse involves the risk of catching cold—a danger that everyone, including the doctors, is aware of. After every bathhouse session the list of people freed from work is lengthened. These are truly ill people, and the doctors know it.

Remember that the wood for the bathhouse is physically carried in on the evening of the previous day on the shoulders of the work gang. Again, this delays returning to the barracks by about two hours and cannot but create an antibathhouse mood.

But that's not all. The worst thing is the obligatory disinfestation chamber.

In camp there is "individual" and "common" underwear; such are the verbal pearls found in official speech. "Individual" underwear is newer and somewhat better and is reserved for trusties, convict foremen, and other privileged persons. No convict has his own underwear. The so-called individual underwear is washed separately and more carefully. It's also replaced more often. "Common" underwear is underwear for anyone. It's handed out in the bathhouse right after bathing in exchange for dirty underwear, which is gathered and counted separately beforehand. There's no opportunity to select anything according to size. Clean underwear is a pure lottery, and I felt a strange and terrible pity at seeing adult men cry over the injustice of receiving worn-out clean underwear in exchange for dirty good underwear. Nothing can take the mind of a human being off the unpleasantries that comprise life. Only vaguely do the convicts realize that, after all, this inconvenience will end the next bathhouse day, that their lives are what's ruined, that there is no reason to worry over some underwear, that they received the old good underwear by chance. But no, they quarrel and cry. This is, of course, a manifestation of those psychoses that are characteristic of a convict's every action, of that same "dementia" which one neuropathologist termed a universal illness.

The spiritual ups and downs of a convict's life have shifted to the point where receiving underwear from a small dark window leading into the depths of the bathhouse is an event that transcends the nerves. Having washed themselves, the men gather at the window far in advance of the actual distribution of underwear. Over and over again they discuss in detail the underwear received last time, the underwear received five years ago at Bamlag. As soon as the board is raised that closes off the small window from within, they rush to it, jostling each other with their slippery, dirty, and stinking bodies.

The underwear is not always dry. Too often it's handed out wet—either there wasn't time enough to dry it or they were short of logs. To put on wet or damp underwear is not a pleasant experience for anyone.

Curses rain down upon the indifferent heads of the men working in the bathhouse. Those who have to put on the damp underwear truly begin to feel the cold, but they must wait for the disinfected outer garments to be handed out.

What exactly is the disinfestation chamber? It is a pit covered with a tarpaulin roof and smeared with clay on the inside. The heat is provided by an iron stove, the mouth of which faces out into the entrance hall. Peacoats, quilted jackets, and pants are hung on poles, the door is tightly shut, and the disinfector begins "laying on the heat." There are no thermometers or bags of sulfur to determine the temperature achieved. Success depends on chance or the diligence of the disinfector.

At best only those things that hang close to the stove are well heated. The remainder, blocked from the heat by the closer items, only get damp. Those in the far corner are taken out cold. No lice are killed by this disinfestation chamber. It's only a formality, and the apparatus has been created for the purpose of tormenting the convict still more.

The doctors understand this very well, but the camp can't be left without a disinfestation chamber. When the prisoners have spent an additional hour waiting in the large dressing room, totally indistinguishable clothing is dragged out by the armful and thrown on the floor. It is up to each person to locate his clothing. The convict swears and dons padded trousers, jacket, and peacoat—all wet from the steam. Afterward, at night, he will sacrifice his last hours of sleep to attempt to dry his clothing at the barracks stove.

It is not hard to understand why no one likes bathhouse day.

Carpenters

>>>

FOR TWO DAYS the white fog was so thick a man couldn't be seen two paces away. But then there wasn't much opportunity to take long walks alone. Somehow you could guess the direction of the mess hall, the hospital, the guard house—those few points we had to be able to find. That same sense of direction that animals possess perfectly also awakens in man under the right conditions.

The men were not shown the thermometer, but that wasn't necessary since they had to work in any weather. Besides, longtime residents of Kolyma could determine the weather precisely even without a thermometer: if there was frosty fog, that meant the temperature outside was forty degrees below zero; if you exhaled easily but in a rasping fashion, it was fifty degrees below zero; if there was a rasping and it was difficult to breathe, it was sixty degrees below; after sixty degrees below zero, spit froze in midair. Spit had been freezing in midair for two weeks.

Potashnikov woke each morning with the hope that the cold had let up during the night. He knew from last winter's experience that no matter how low the temperature was, a sharp change was necessary for a feeling of warmth. If the frost were to weaken its grip even to forty or fifty degrees below zero, it would be warm for two days, and there was no sense in planning more than two days ahead.

But the cold kept up, and Potashnikov knew he couldn't hold out any longer. Breakfast sustained his strength for no more than an hour of work, and then exhaustion ensued. Frost penetrated the body to the "marrow of the bone"—the phrase was no metaphor. A man could wave his pick or shovel, jump up and down so as not to freeze—till dinner. Dinner was hot—a thin broth and two spoons of kasha that restored one's strength only a little but nevertheless provided some warmth. And then there was strength to work for an hour, and after that Potashnikov again felt himself in the grip of the cold. The day would finally come to a close, and after supper all the workers would take their bread back to the barracks, where they would eat it, washing it down with a mug of hot water. Not a single man would eat his bread in the mess hall with his soup. After that Potashnikov would go to sleep.

He slept, of course, on one of the upper berths, because the lower ones were like an ice cellar. Everyone who had a lower berth would stand half the night at the stove, taking turns with his neighbors in embracing it; the stove retained a slight remnant of warmth. There was never enough firewood, because to go for it meant a four-kilometer walk after work and everyone avoided the task. The upper berths were warmer, but even so everyone slept in his working clothes—hats, padded coats, pea jackets, felt pants. Even with the extra warmth, by the morning a man's hair would be frozen to the pillow.

Potashnikov felt his strength leaving him every day. A thirty-year-old man, he had difficulty in climbing onto an upper berth and even in getting down from it. His neighbor had died yesterday. The man simply didn't wake up, and no one asked for the cause of death, as if there were only one cause that everyone knew. The orderly was happy that the man died in the morning, and not in the evening, since the orderly got the dead man's ration for the day. Everyone realized this, and Potashnikov screwed up his courage to approach the orderly.

"Break off a piece of the crust," he asked, but the orderly cursed him as only a man whose weakness lent him strength could. Potashnikov fell silent and walked away.

He had to take some action, think of something with his weakened mind. Either that or die. Potashnikov had no fear of death, but he couldn't rid himself of a passionate secret desire,

a last stubbornness—to live. He didn't want to die here in the
frost under the boots of the guards, in the barracks with its
swearing, dirt, and total indifference written on every face. He
bore no grudge for people's indifference, for he had long since
comprehended the source of that spiritual dullness. The same
frost that transformed a man's spit into ice in midair also penetrated the soul. If bones could freeze, then the brain could also
be dulled and the soul could freeze over. And the soul shuddered and froze—perhaps to remain frozen forever. Potashnikov had lost everything except the desire to survive, to
endure the cold and remain alive.

Having gulped down his bowl of warm soup, Potashnikov
was barely able to drag himself to the work area. The work
gang stood at attention before beginning work, and a fat redfaced man in a deerskin hat and a white leather coat walked
up and down the rows in Yakut deerskin boots. He peered into
their exhausted dirty faces. The gang foreman walked up and
respectfully spoke to the man in the deerskin hat.

"I really haven't got anyone like that, Alexander Yevgenievich. You'll have to try Sobolev and the petty criminal element. These are all intellectuals, Alexander Yevgenievich.
They're a pain in the neck."

The man in the deerskin hat stopped looking over the
men and turned to the gang foreman.

"The foremen don't know their people, they don't want to
know, they don't want to help us," he said hoarsely.

"Have it your way, Alexander Yevgenievich."

"I'll show you. What's your name?"

"My name's Ivanov, Alexander Yevgenievich."

"Just watch. Hey, guys, attention!" The man in the deerskin hat walked up to the work gang. "The camp administration needs carpenters to make boxes to haul dirt."

Everyone was silent.

"You see, Alexander Yevgenievich?" the foreman whispered.

Potashnikov suddenly heard his own voice.

"I'm a carpenter." And he stepped forward. Another man stepped forward on his right. Potashnikov knew him; it was Grigoriev.

"Well," said the man in the deerskin hat, turning to the foreman, "are you an incompetent asshole or not? Okay, fellows, follow me."

Potashnikov and Grigoriev stumbled after the man in the deerskin hat. He stopped.

"At this pace," he said hoarsely, "we won't make it even by dinnertime. Here's what. I'll go ahead and you go to the shop and ask for the foreman, Sergeev. You know where the carpentry shop is?"

"We know, we know," Grigoriev said in a loud voice. "Please, give us a smoke."

"I think I've heard that request before," the man in the deerskin hat muttered and pulled out two cigarettes without removing the pack from his pocket.

Potashnikov walked ahead and thought frantically. Today he would be in the warmth of the carpentry shop. He'd sharpen the ax and make a handle. And sharpen the saw. No sense hurrying. He could kill time till dinner signing out the tools and finding the quartermaster. By evening they'd realize he didn't know how to make an ax handle or sharpen a saw, and they'd kick him out. Tomorrow he'd have to return to the work gang. But today he'd be warm. Maybe he could remain a carpenter tomorrow and the day after tomorrow—if Grigoriev was a carpenter. He'd be Grigoriev's helper. Winter was nearly over. Somehow he'd survive the short summer.

Potashnikov stopped and waited for Grigoriev.

"Do you know how . . . to be a carpenter?" he asked, holding his breath in sudden hope.

"Well, you see," said Grigoriev cheerfully, "I was a graduate student at the Moscow Philological Institute. I don't see why anyone with a higher education, especially one in the humanities, can't sharpen an ax and set the teeth on a saw. Particularly if he has to do it next to a hot stove."

"That means you can't do it either. . . ."

"It doesn't mean anything. We'll fool them for two days, and what do you care what happens after that?"

"We'll fool them for one day, and tomorrow we'll be back in the work gang. . . ."

Together the two of them barely managed to open the frozen door. In the middle of the carpentry shop stood a red-hot cast-iron stove; five carpenters were working without coats and hats at their benches. The new arrivals knelt before the stove's open door as if it were the god of fire, one of man's first gods. They threw down their mittens and stretched their hands toward the warmth but were not able to feel it immediately since their hands were numb. In a minute Grigoriev and Potashnikov knelt, took off their hats, and unbuttoned their padded jackets.

"What are you doing here?" one of the carpenters asked with hostility.

"We're carpenters. We're going to work here," Grigoriev said.

"Alexander Yevgenievich said so," Potashnikov added hurriedly.

"That means you're the ones the foreman told us to give axes to?" asked Arishtrem, an older man in charge of tools who was planing shovel handles in the corner.

"That's us, that's us. . . ."

"Here they are," Arishtrem said, looking them over sceptically. "Two axes, a saw, and a tooth setter. You'll return the tooth setter later. Here's my ax; make yourself a handle with it."

Arishtrem smiled.

"You'll have to do thirty handles a day," he said.

Grigoriev took the block of wood from Arishtrem's hands and began to hack away at it. The dinner horn sounded, but Arishtrem kept staring silently at Grigoriev's work.

"Now you," he said to Potashnikov.

Potashnikov put the log on the stump, took the ax from Grigoriev's hands, and began to trim the piece.

The carpenters had all left for dinner, and there was no one left in the shop except the three men.

"Take my two ax handles," Arishtrem said, handing the two ready pieces to Grigoriev, "and mount the heads. Sharpen the saw. You can stay warm at the stove today and tomorrow. After that, go back where you came from. Here's a piece of bread for dinner."

They stayed warm at the stove those two days, and the following day it was only twenty degrees below zero. Winter was over.

PART TWO

HOPE

Dry Rations

>>>

WHEN THE FOUR of us reached the mountain spring "Dus-kania," we were so happy we virtually stopped talking to each other. We feared that our trip here was someone's joke or mistake and that we would be returned to plod through the icy waters at the gold mine's stone face. Our feet had been frost-bitten a number of times, and our regulation-issue galoshes couldn't protect them from the cold.

We followed the tractor prints as if we were hunting some enormous prehistoric beast, but the tractor road came to an end and we continued along an old, barely distinguishable footpath. We reached a small log cabin with two windows and a door hanging on a hinge that was cut from an automobile tire and nailed to the doorway. The small door had an enormous handle that looked like the handles on restaurant doors in big towns. Inside were cots made of slender logs. On the earthen floor lay a smoky black tin can. All around the small moss-covered cabin lay other rusty yellow cans of the same sort. The hut belonged to the geological prospecting group; more than a year had passed since anyone had lived in it. We were to live here and cut a road through the forest. We had brought saws and axes with us.

It was the first time we had received our food ration in advance. I was carrying a small cherished bag containing grain, sugar, fish, and some lard. The bag was tied in several places with bits of twine like a sausage. Savelev had a similar sack, but Ivan Ivanovich had two of them sewn with large masculine stitches. The fourth, Fedya Shapov, had poured his grain frivolously into the pockets of his jacket and used a knotted foot rag that served us instead of socks to hold his sugar. He'd ripped out the inner pocket of the pea jacket for a tobacco pouch in which he carefully stored any cigarette butts he happened to come across.

The very thought that this tiny ten-day ration had to be divided into thirty parts was frightening. Of course, we had the choice of eating twice a day instead of three times. We'd taken bread for only two days, since the foreman would be bringing it to us. Even such a small group was unthinkable without a foreman. We were totally unconcerned with who he might be. We'd been told that we had to prepare our quarters before he arrived.

We were all tired of barracks food. Each time they brought in the soup in large zinc tubs suspended on poles, it made us all want to cry. We were ready to cry for fear that the soup would be thin. And when a miracle occurred and the soup was thick, we couldn't believe it and ate it as slowly as possible. But even with thick soup in a warm stomach there remained a sucking pain; we'd been hungry for too long. All human emotions—love, friendship, envy, concern for one's fellow man, compassion, longing for fame, honesty—had left us with the flesh that had melted from our bodies during their long fasts.

Savelev and I decided to eat separately. The preparation of food is a special joy for a convict. To prepare food with one's own hands and then eat it was an incomparable pleasure, even if the skilled hands of a cook might have done it better. Our culinary skills were insignificant, and we didn't know how to prepare even a simple soup or kasha. Nevertheless, Savelev and I gathered up the cans, washed them, burned them on the campfire, cooked, fussed, and learned from each other.

Ivan Ivanovich and Fedya combined their food. Fedya emptied his pockets carefully, examining each stitch, cleaning out the individual grains with a grimy broken fingernail.

We, the four of us, were quite prepared for a trip into the future—either into the sky or into the earth. We were all well aware of the nature of scientifically determined food rations, of how certain types of food were brought in to replace others, and how a bucket of water was considered the equivalent in calories of a quarter pound of butter. We'd all learned meekness and had forgotten how to be surprised. We had no pride, vanity, or ambition, and jealousy and passion seemed as alien to us as Mars, and trivial in addition. It was much more important to learn to button your pants in the frost. Grown men cried if they weren't able to do that. We understood that death was no worse than life, and we feared neither. We were overwhelmed by indifference. We knew that it was in our power to end this life the very next day and now and again we made that decision, but each time life's trivia would interfere with our plans. Today they would promise an extra kilo of bread as a reward for good work, and it would be simply foolish to commit suicide on such a day. The following time the orderly of the next barracks would promise a smoke to pay back an old debt.

We realized that life, even the worst life, consists of an alternation of joys and sorrows, successes and failures, and there was no need to fear the failures more than the successes.

We were disciplined and obedient to our superiors. We understood that truth and falsehood were sisters and that there were thousands of truths in the world. . . . We considered ourselves virtual saints, since we had redeemed all our sins by our years in camp. We had learned to understand people, to foresee their actions and fathom them. We had learned—and this was the most important thing—that our knowledge of people did not provide us with anything useful in life. What did it matter if I understood, felt, foresaw the actions of another person? I was powerless to change my own attitude toward him, and I couldn't denounce a fellow convict, no matter what he did. I refused to seek the job of foreman, which provided a chance to remain alive, for the worst thing in a camp was the forcing of one's own or anyone else's will on another person who was a convict just like oneself. I refused to seek "useful" acquaintanceships, to give bribes. And what good did it do to know that Ivanov was a scoundrel, that Petrov was a spy, or that Zaslavsky had given false testimony?

Our inability to use certain types of "weapons" weakened us in comparison with certain of our neighbors who shared berths with us. We learned to be satisfied with little things and rejoice at small successes.

We learned one other amazing thing: in the eyes of the state and its representatives a physically strong person was better—yes, better—more moral, more valuable than a weak person who couldn't shovel twenty cubic meters of dirt out of a trench in a day. The former was more moral than the latter. He fulfilled his "quota," that is, carried out his chief duty to the state and society and was therefore respected by all. His advice was asked and his desires were taken into consideration, he was invited to meetings whose topics were far removed from shovelling heavy slippery dirt from wet and slimy ditches.

Thanks to his physical advantages, such a person was transformed into a moral force in the resolution of the numerous everyday questions of camp life. Of course, he remained a moral force only as long as he remained a physical force.

When Ivan Ivanovich was first brought to camp he was an excellent "worker." Now that he had become weak from hunger, he was unable to understand why everyone beat him in passing. He wasn't beaten severely, but he was beaten: by the orderly, the barber, the contractor, the group leader, the work gang leader, the guard. Aside from these camp officials, he was also beaten by the camp criminals. Ivan Ivanovich was happy that he had been included in our group.

Fedya Shapov, a teenager from the Altai region, became physically exhausted before the others did because his half-grown body was still not very strong. He was the only son of a widow, and he was convicted of illegal livestock slaughter. He had slaughtered a sheep—an act punishable by a ten-year sentence. Accustomed as he was to farm work, he found the fran-

tic labor of the camp particularly difficult. Fedya admired the
free life of the criminal element in camp, but there was something in his nature that kept him from becoming close to the
thieves. His healthy peasant upbringing and love—rather than
revulsion—for work helped him a little. The youngest among
us, he immediately became attached to our oldest and most
decent member—Ivan Ivanovich.

Savelev had been a student in the Moscow Telegraph Institute and later was my fellow inmate in Butyr Prison. As a
loyal member of the Young Communist League, he was
shaken by all he had seen and he had written a letter to the
party "leader," since he was convinced that someone must be
keeping such information from the "leader." His own case was
so trivial (writing letters to his fiancée) that the only proof of
agitation (Article 58, Point 10) consisted of their corre-
spondence. His "organization" (Point 11 of the same article)
consisted of two persons. All this was noted down in dead
seriousness on the interrogation forms. Nevertheless, even in
view of the then prevalent scale of offenses, no one believed he
would be condemned to anything more than exile.

Soon after sending the letter on one of the days officially
designated for petitions, Savelev was called out into the corridor and given a notice to sign. The supreme prosecutor in-
formed him that he would personally examine his case. After
that Savelev was summoned on only one other occasion, to be
handed the sentence of the "Special Council"—ten years in
the camps.

In camp Savelev was rapidly reduced to a shade of his
former self, but even then he could not comprehend the sinister punishment meted out to him. The two of us couldn't
have been called friends; we simply loved to remember Moscow together—her streets and monuments, the Moscow River
with its thin layer of oil that glistened like mother-of-pearl.
Neither Leningrad, Kiev, nor Odessa could boast of such passionate devotees. The two of us could talk endlessly of Moscow. . . .

We set up the iron stove that we had brought with us in the cabin and, although it was summer, lit a fire. The warm dry air was wonderfully aromatic. We were all accustomed to breathing the sour smells of old clothing and sweat. It was a good thing that tears have no odor.

On the advice of Ivan Ivanovich, we took off our underwear and buried it in the ground overnight. Each undershirt and pair of shorts was buried separately with only a small piece protruding above the ground. This was a folk remedy against lice. Back at the mine we had been helpless against them. In the morning we discovered that the lice really had gathered on the protruding bits of shirt. Although the land here lay under the permafrost, it nevertheless thawed sufficiently in the summer for us to bury the articles of underwear. Of course, the soil in this area contained more stones than dirt. But even from this soil of ice and stone there grew up dense pine forests with tree trunks so wide that it took three men with outstretched arms to span them. Such was the life force of the trees—a magnificent lesson given to us by nature.

We burned the lice, holding the shirts up to the burning logs of the fire. Unfortunately this clever method did not destroy the parasites and on the very same day we boiled our underwear furiously in large tin cans. This time the method of disinfection was a reliable one.

It was later, in hunting mice, crows, seagulls, and squirrels, that we learned the magic qualities of the earth. The flesh of any animal loses its particular odor if it is first buried in the ground.

We took every precaution to keep our fire from going out, since we had only a few matches that were kept by Ivan Ivanovich. He wrapped the precious matches in a piece of canvas and then in rags as carefully as possible.

Each evening we would lay two logs on the fire, and they would smoulder till morning without either flaming up or going out. Three logs would have burned up. Savelev and I had learned that truth at our school desks, but Ivan Ivanovich and Fedya had learned it as children at home. In the morning we would separate the logs. They would flare up with a yellow flame, and we would throw a heavy log on top.

I divided the grain into ten parts, but that was too alarming an operation. It was probably easier to feed ten thousand people with five loaves than for a convict to divide his ten-day ration into thirty parts. Ration cards were always based on a ten-day period. The ten-day system had long since died out on the "mainland," but here it was maintained on a permanent basis. No one here saw any need for Sunday holidays or for the convicts to have "rest days."

Unable to bear this torment, I mixed all the grain together and asked Ivan Ivanovich and Fedya to let me come in with them. I turned all my food into the common pot, and Savelev followed my example.

The four of us made a wise decision—to cook just twice a day. There simply weren't enough provisions for three meals.

"We'll gather fruits and mushrooms," said Ivan Ivanovich. "We can catch mice and birds. And one or two days in every ten we can live on bread alone."

"But if we're to go hungry for one or two days every time we expect a food delivery," said Savelev, "then how will we be able to resist overeating when the stuff is actually brought?"

We decided to make the food as watery as possible and to eat only twice a day—no matter what. After all, no one would steal from us. We had all received our supplies intact, and we had no drunken cooks, thieving quartermasters, greedy overseers, criminals to take the best pieces, or any of that endless horde of administrators who without fear or any trace of control or conscience were able to pick the convict clean.

We had received all our "fats" in the form of a lump of watery fat, some sugar—less than the amount of gold that I was able to pan—and sticky bread created by the inimitable experts of the heavy thumb who fed the administrators of the bakery. There were twenty different kinds of grain that we had never heard of in the entire course of our lives. It was all too mysterious. And frightening.

The fish that was to take the place of meat according to the "replacement tables" was half-spoiled herring intended to replenish our intensified expenditure of protein.

Alas, even the full ration we had received could not feed us or fill our bellies. We required three times, four times as much, for our bodies had gone hungry for too long. We did not understand this simple truth. We believed in the "norms," and we had never heard the well-known remark made by all cooks—that it is easier to cook for twenty persons than for four. We understood one thing clearly: that we would not have enough food. This did not so much frighten as surprise us. We had to begin work and start cutting a road through the undergrowth and fallen trees.

Trees in the north die lying down—like people. Their enormous bared roots look like the claws of a monstrous predatory bird that has seized onto a rock. Downward from these gigantic claws to the permafrost stretch thousands of tiny tentacles, whitish shoots covered with warm brown bark. Each summer the permafrost retreats a little and each inch of thawed soil is immediately pierced by a root shoot that digs in with its fine tendrils. The first reach maturity in three hundred years, slowly hoisting their heavy, powerful bodies on these weak roots scattered flat over the stony soil. A strong wind easily topples these trees that stand on such frail feet. The trees fall on their backs, their heads pointed away from their feet, and die lying on a soft thick layer of moss that is either bright green or crimson.

Only the shorter twisted trees, tormented from following a constantly shifting sun and warmth, manage to stand firm and distant from each other. They have kept up such an intense struggle for existence for so long that their tortured, gnarled wood is worthless. The short knotty trunk entwined with terrible growths like splints on broken bones could not be used for construction even in the north, which was not fussy about ma-

terials. These twisted trees could not be used even as firewood; so well did they resist the ax, they would have exhausted any worker. Thus did they take vengeance for their
broken northern lives.

Our task was to clear a road, and we boldly set about our
work. We sawed from sunrise to sundown, felled and stacked
trees. Wanting to stay here as long as possible and fearing the
gold mines, we forgot about everything. The stacks grew
slowly and by the end of the second difficult day it became evident that we had accomplished little, but were incapable of
doing more. Ivan Ivanovich measured the distance from the
tip of his thumb to the tip of his middle finger five times along
a ten-year old pine to make a one-meter measuring stick.

In the evening the foreman came to measure our work
with his notched staff and shook his head. We had accomplished 10 percent of the norm!

Ivan Ivanovich tried to make his point and justify our
measurements, but the foreman was unyielding. He muttered
something about "cubic meters" and "density." And although
we were not familiar with the technical methods of measuring
wood production, one thing was clear. We would be returned
to the camp zone where we would again pass through the
gates with their inscription: "Work is honorable, glorious, val-
iant, and heroic."

In the camp we learned to hate physical labor and work in
general.

But we were not afraid. More than that: the foreman's as-
sessment of our work and physical capacity as hopeless and
worthless brought us a feeling of unheard-of-relief and was
not at all frightening.

We realized we were at the end of our rope, and we simply
let matters take their course. Nothing bothered us any more,
and we breathed freely in the fist of another man's will. We
didn't even concern ourselves with staying alive, and ate and
slept on the same schedule as in camp. Our spiritual calm,
achieved by a dulling of the senses, was reminiscent of the

"dungeon's supreme freedom" and Tolstoy's nonresistance to evil. Our spiritual calm was always guarded by our subordination to another's will.

We had long since given up planning our lives more than a day in advance.

The foreman left and we remained to cut a road through the forest and erect new log stacks, but now we did so with greater peace of mind and indifference. We stopped quarrelling over who would take the heavy end when we stacked logs.

We rested more and paid more attention to the sun, the forest, and the pale-blue tall sky. We loafed.

In the morning Savelev and I somehow felled an enormous black pine that had miraculously survived both storm and forest fire. We tossed the saw into the grass. It rang out, striking a stone, and we sat down on the trunk of the fallen tree.

"Just imagine," said Savelev. "We'll survive, leave for the mainland, and quickly become sick old men. We'll have heart pains and rheumatism, and all the sleepless nights, the hunger, and long hard work of our youth will leave their mark on us even if we remain alive. We'll be sick without knowing why, groan and drag ourselves from one dispensary to another. This unbearable work will leave us with wounds that can't be healed, and all our later years will lead to lives of physical and psychological pain. And that pain will be endless and assume many different forms. But even among those terrible future days there will be good ones when we'll be almost healthy and we won't think about our sufferings. And the number of those days will be exactly equal to the number of days each of us has been able to loaf in camp."

"But how about 'honest work'?" I asked.

"The only ones who call for honest work are the bastards who beat and maim us, eat our food, and force us living skeletons to work to our very deaths. It's profitable for them, but they believe in 'honest work' even less than we do."

In the evening we sat around our precious stove, and Fedya Shapov listened attentively to Savelev's hoarse voice:

"Well, he refused to work. They made up a report, said he was dressed appropriately for the season. . . ."

"What does that mean—'appropriately for the season'?" asked Fedya.

"Well, they can't list every piece of summer or winter clothing you have on. If it's in the winter, they can't write that you were sent to work without a coat or mittens. How often did you stay in camp because there were not mittens?"

"Never," Fedya said timidly. "The boss made us stamp down the snow on the road. Or esle they would have had to write that we stayed beyond because we didn't have anything to wear."

"There you have it."

"Okay, tell me about the subway."

And Savelev would tell Fedya about the Moscow subway. Ivan Ivanovich and I also liked to listen to Savelev, since he knew things that I had never guessed, although I had lived in Moscow.

"Muslims, Fedya," said Savelev, delighted that he could still think clearly, "are called to worship by a muezzin from the minaret. Muhammed chose the human voice as a signal to prayer. Muhammed tried everything—trumpets, tambourines, signal fires; nothing pleased him. . . . Fifteen hundred years later when they were choosing a signal to start the subway trains, it turned out that neither the whistle, nor the horn, nor the siren could be heard as easily by the train engineer's ear— with the same precision—as the live voice of the dispatcher on duty shouting "Ready!"

Fedya gasped with delight. He was better adapted than any of us to the forest, more experienced than any of us in spite of his youth. Fedya could do carpentry work, build a simple cabin in the taiga, fell a tree and use its branches to make a shelter. In addition, Fedya was a hunter; in his locality people were used to guns from childhood. But cold and hunger wiped out Fedya's qualities, and the earth ignored his knowledge and abilities. Fedya did not envy city dwellers, but simply acknowledged their superiority and could listen endlessly to their stories of the wonders of science and the miracles of the city.

Friendship is not born in conditions of need or trouble. Literary fairy tales tell of "difficult" conditions which are an essential element in forming any friendship, but such conditions are simply not difficult enough. If tragedy and need brought people together and gave birth to their friendship, then the need was not extreme and the tragedy not great. Tragedy is not deep and sharp if it can be shared with friends. Only real need can determine one's spiritual and physical strength and set the limits of one's physical endurance and moral courage.

We all understood that we could survive only through luck. Strangely enough, in my youth whenever I experienced failure I used to repeat the saying: "Well, at least we won't die from hunger." It never crossed my mind to doubt the truth of this sentence. And at the age of thirty I found myself in a very real sense dying from hunger and literally fighting for a piece of bread. And this was a long time before the war.

When the four of us gathered at the spring "Duskania," we all knew we had not gathered through friendship. We all knew that if we survived we would not want to meet again. It would be painful to remember the insane hunger, the unchecked gastronomic lies at the fire, our quarrels with each other and our identical dreams. All of us had the same dreams of loaves of rye bread that flew past us like meteors or angels.

A human being survives by his ability to forget. Memory is always ready to blot out the bad and retain only the good. There was nothing good at the spring "Duskania," and nothing good was either expected in the future or remembered in the past by any of us. We had all been permanently poisoned by the north, and we knew it. Three of us stopped resisting

fate, and only Ivan Ivanovich kept working with the same
tragic diligence as before.

Savelev tried to reason with Ivan Ivanovich during one of
the smoking breaks. For us it was just an ordinary rest period
for nonsmokers since we hadn't had any homemade tobacco
for a number of years. Still we held to the breaks. In the taiga,
smokers would gather and dry black-currant leaves, and there
were heated convict discussions as to whether cowberry
leaves or currant leaves were better. Experts maintained that
both were worthless, since the body demands the poison of
nicotine, not smoke, and brain cells could not be tricked by
such a simple method. But currant leaf served for our "smoking breaks," since in camp the words "rest from work" pre-
sented too glaring a contradiction with the basic principles of
production ethics held in the far north. To rest every hour was
both a challenge and a crime, and dried currant leaf was a nat-
ural camouflage.

"Listen, Ivan," said Savelev. "I'll tell you a story. In Bamlag, we were working on the side track and hauling sand in
wheelbarrows. It was a long distance, and we had to put out
twenty-five meters a day. If you didn't fill your quota, your
bread ration got cut to three hundred grams. Soup once a day.
Whoever filled the quota got an extra kilo of bread and could
buy a second kilo in the store if he had the cash. We worked in
pairs. But the quotas were impossible. So here's what we did:
one day we'd work for you from your trench and fill the quota.
We'd get two kilos of bread plus your three hundred grams. So
we'd each get one kilo, one hundred and fifty grams. The next
day we'd work for my quota. Then for yours. We did it for a
month, and it wasn't a bad life. Luckily for us the foreman was
a decent sort, since he knew what was up. It worked out well
even for him. His men kept up their strength and production
didn't drop. Then someone higher up figured things out, and
our luck came to an end."

"How about trying it here?" said Ivan Ivanovich.

"I don't want to, but we'll help you out."

"How about you?"

"We couldn't care less, friend."

"I guess I don't care either. Let's just wait for the foreman to come."

The foreman arrived in a few days, and our worst fears were realized.

"Okay, you've had your rest. Your time is up. Might as well give someone else a chance. This has been a bit like a sanatorium or maybe a health club for you," the foreman joked without cracking a smile.

"I guess so," said Savelev:

> *First you go to the club*
> *And then off to play;*
> *Tie a tag to your toe*
> *And jump in your grave.*

We pretended to laugh, out of politeness.

"When do we go back?"

"Tomorrow."

Ivan Ivanovich didn't ask any more questions. He hanged himself that night ten paces from the cabin in the tree fork without even using a rope. I'd never seen that kind of suicide before. Savelev found him, saw him from the path and let out a yell. The foreman came running, ordered us not to take him down until the investigating group arrived, and hurried us off.

Fedya Shapov and I didn't know what to do—Ivan Ivanovich had some good foot rags that weren't torn. He also had some sacks, a calico shirt that he boiled to remove the lice, and some patched felt boots. His padded jacket lay on his bunk. We talked it over briefly and took the things for ourselves. Savelev didn't take part in the division of the dead man's clothing. He just kept walking around Ivan Ivanovich's body. In the world of free men a body always and everywhere stimulates a vague interest, attracts like a magnet. This is not the case either in war or in the camps, where the everyday nature of death and the deadening of feeling kills any interest in a dead body. But Savelev was struck by Ivan Ivanovich's death. It had stirred up and lit some dark corners of his soul, and forced him to make decisions of his own.

He walked into the cabin, took the ax from one corner, and stepped back over the threshold. The foreman, who had been sitting on a mound of earth piled around the cabin, jumped up and began to shout something. Fedya and I ran out into the yard.

Savelev walked up to the thick, short pine log on which we had always sawed wood. The surface was scarred by the ax, and the bark had all been chopped off. He put his left hand on the log, spread the fingers, and swung the ax.

The foreman squealed shrilly. Fedya ran toward Savelev, but the four fingers had already flown into the sawdust. At first we couldn't even see them among the branches and fine chips. Crimson blood surged from the stump of Savelev's hand. Fedya and I ripped up Ivan Ivanovich's shirt, applied the tourniquet, and bound the wound.

The foreman took us back to camp. Savelev was sent to the first-aid point and from there to Investigations to be tried on a charge of self-mutilation. Fedya and I returned to that same tent which we had left two weeks before with such hopes and expectations of happiness.

The upper berths were already occupied by others, but we didn't care, since it was summer and even better to be lower down. There would be a lot of changes by winter.

I fell asleep quickly, but woke up in the middle of the night. I walked up to the table of the orderly on duty where Fedya was sitting with a sheet of paper in his hand. Over his shoulder I could read:

"Mama," Fedya wrote, "Mama, I'm all right. Mama, I'm dressed appropriately for the season. . . ."

Sententious

Dedicated to Nadezhda Mandelshtam

PEOPLE MATERIALIZED out of nowhere—one after another. A stranger would lie down next to me on my berth and nestle against my bony shoulder in the night, giving me his pitiful warmth and receiving my own in exchange. There were nights when no warmth at all penetrated the rags of my pea jacket and padded vest, and in the morning I would think my neighbor was dead and be surprised that he would rise in response to a shouted command, get dressed, and submissively obey the order. I had little warmth. Little flesh was left on my bones, just enough for bitterness—the last human emotion; it was closer to the the bone. The man who had appeared from nowhere would disappear forever in the day, for there were many work areas for coal prospecting. I didn't know the people who slept at my side. I never asked them questions. There is an Arab saying: "He who asks no questions will be told no lies." That wasn't the case here. I couldn't have cared less if I was being told lies or the truth. The camp criminals have a cruel saying which is even more appropriate here—it expresses a deep contempt for the questioner: "If you don't believe it, take it as a fairy tale." I neither asked questions nor listened to fairytales.

What remained with me till the very end? Bitterness. And I expected this bitterness to stay with me till death. But death, just recently so near, began to ease away little by little. Death was replaced not by life, but by semiconsciousness, an existence which had no formula and could not be called life. Each day, each sunrise brought with it the danger of some new lurch into death. But it never happened. I had the easiest of jobs, easier even than being a watchman—I chopped wood to boil water. They could have kicked me out, but where to? The taiga is a distant thing, and our little village was like an island in the world of the taiga. I could barely lift my feet, the two hundred yards from the tent to the work area seemed endless, and to cover it I had to rest more than once. Even now I clearly remember all the ruts and potholes on that path of death. And I remember the creek on whose bank I would lie on my stomach to lap up the cold, delicious water. The two-handed saw that I sometimes carried on my shoulder and sometimes dragged behind me seemed unbelievably heavy.

I never did manage to boil water in time for dinner. But none of the workers (all of them had been convicts just yesterday) ever noticed if the water was boiling or not. Kolyma had taught all of us to distinguish only hot water from cold, raw water.

We were totally indifferent about the dialectic leap of quantity into quality. We weren't philosophers but workers, and our hot drinking water betrayed none of the important qualities of this leap.

I ate, indifferently stuffing into my mouth anything that seemed edible—scraps, last year's marsh berries.

There were two shotguns in our tent. Grouse were not afraid of people and at first they could be shot from the tent threshold itself. Game was either roasted whole in the ashes of the campfire or it was boiled. Down for pillows was a sure source of income for the free masters of guns and forest birds. Cleaned and plucked, the birds were boiled in three-quart tin cans suspended over the campfire. I never found any remnants of these magic birds. The hungry teeth of free men ground each bone to nothing. This was another miracle of the taiga.

I never tried a piece of grouse. Mine were the berries, the roots of the grass, the rations. And I didn't die. With increasing indifference and without bitterness I began to watch the cold red sun, the bare mountaintops where the rocks, the turns of the river, the trees were all sharp and unfriendly. In the evenings a cold fog rose from the river, and there was no single hour in the taiga day when I felt warm.

My frostbitten fingers and toes ached, hummed from the pain. The bright skin of the fingers remained rosy and sensitive. I kept my fingers wrapped in any kind of dirty rag to protect them from a new wound, from pain, but not from infection. Pus seeped endlessly from both my big toes.

I was awakened by a hammer blow on the rail, and a blow on the rails also marked the end of the day. After supper I would immediately lie down on my bunk without undressing and, naturally, fall asleep. I perceived the tent in which I lived as if through a fog; people moved back and forth, loud swearing could be heard, there were fights interrupted by sudden silence before a dangerous blow. Fights died down quickly of their own accord. No one held anyone back, no one separated anyone. The motor of aggression simply died out, and there ensued the cold silence of night with a pale tall sky peering through the holes of the canvas, and all around were groans, snoring, wheezing, coughing, and the mindless swearing of sleeping men.

Once at night I suddenly realized that I heard groans and wheezing. The sensation was as sudden as the dawn and did not gladden me. Later, as I recollected this moment of amazement, I understood that the need for sleep, forgetfulness, unconsciousness had lessened. I'd "woken up," as Moses Kuznetsov used to say. He was a blacksmith and a clever, intelligent man.

There appeared an insistent pain in the muscles. I can't imagine what sort of muscles I could have had, but they did ache and enrage me by not letting me forget about my body. Then something else appeared—something different from resentment and bitterness. There appeared indifference and fearlessness. I realized I didn't care if I was to be beaten or not, given dinner and the daily "ration" or not. The prospecting group was not guarded, so there was no one to beat me as in the mines. Nevertheless, I remembered the mine and measured my courage by its rule. This indifference and lack of fear cast a sort of bridge over to death. The realization that there would be no beatings here, that they didn't beat you here, gave birth to new feelings, new strength.

Later came fear, not a strong fear, but nevertheless a fear of losing the salvation of this life and work, of losing the tall cold sky and the aching pain in worn-out muscles. I realized I was afraid of leaving here for the mines. I was afraid and that was all there was to it. I had never striven to improve my life if I was content with it. The flesh on my bones grew every day. Envy was the name of the next feeling that returned to me. I envied my dead friends who had died in '38. I envied those of my neighbors who had something to chew or smoke. I didn't envy the camp chief, the foreman, the work brigade leader; that was a different world altogether.

Love didn't return to me. Oh, how distant is love from envy, from fear, from bitterness. How little people need love. Love comes only when all other human emotions have already returned. Love comes last, returns last. Or does it return? Indifference, envy, and fear, however, were not the only witnesses of my return to life. Pity for animals returned earlier than pity for people.

As the weakest in this world of excavations and exploratory ditches, I worked with the topographer, dragging his rod and theodolite. Sometimes, to be able to move faster, the topographer would strap the theodolite to his own back and leave me with only the light rod painted all over with numbers. The topographer was a former convict himself. That summer there were a number of escaped convicts in the taiga, and the topographer asked for and received a small-caliber rifle from the camp authorities. But the rifle only interfered with our work. And not just because it was an extra thing to carry in our difficult travels. Once we sat down to rest, and the topographer took aim at a red-breasted bullfinch that had flown up to look us over and lure us away from the nest. If necessary, the bird was ready to sacrifice its life. The female must have been sitting on eggs somewhere near for him to have been so insanely bold. The topographer threw up the rifle, but I pushed the barrel away.

"Put away the gun!"

"What's the matter with you? Are you crazy?"

"Leave the bird alone."

"I'll report this to the chief."

"The hell with your chief."

But the topographer didn't want to quarrel and didn't report the incident. I realized that something important had returned to me.

I hadn't seen newspapers or books for years, and I had long since trained myself not to regret the loss. All fifty-five of my neighbors in the torn tarpaulin tent felt the same way. There was no book or newspaper in our barracks. The camp authorities—the foreman, the chief of prospecting, the superintendant—had descended into our world without books.

My language was the crude language of the mines and it was as impoverished as the emotions that lived near the bones. Get up, go to work, dinner, end of work, rest, citizen chief, may I speak, shovel, trench, yes sir, drill, pick, it's cold outside, rain, cold soup, hot soup, bread, ration, leave me the butt—these few dozen words were all I had needed for years. Half of them were obscenities. The wealth of Russian profanity, its inexhaustible offensiveness, was not revealed to me either in my childhood or in my youth. But I did not seek other words. I was happy that I did not have to search for other words. I didn't even know if they existed. I couldn't have answered that question.

I was frightened, shaken when there appeared in my brain (I clearly remember that it was in the back of the skull) a word totally inappropriate for the taiga, a word which I didn't myself understand, not to mention my comrades. I shouted out the word:

"Sententious! Sententious!"

I roared with laughter.

"Sententious!" I shouted directly into the northern sky, into the double dawn, still not understanding the meaning of the word that had been born within me. And if the word had returned, then all the better! A great joy filled me.

"Sententious!"

"Idiot!"

"He really is! What are you, a foreigner or something?" The question was asked ironically by Vronsky. The very same Vronsky, the mountain engineer. Three shreds.

"Vronsky, give me a smoke."

"Can't, haven't got anything."

"Just three shreds of tobacco."

"Three shreds? Okay."

From a tobacco pouch stuffed with homemade tobacco a dirty fingernail extracted three shreds of tobacco.

"A foreigner?" The question shifted our fate into the world of provocations and denunciations, investigations and lengthened sentences.

But I couldn't care less about Vronsky's question. The find was enormous.

Bitterness was the last feeling with which man departed into nonbeing, into the world of the dead. But was it dead? Even a stone didn't seem dead to me, not to mention the grass, the trees, the river. The river was not only the incarnation of life, not just a symbol of life, but life itself. It possessed eternal movement, calm, a silent and secret language of its own, its business that forced it to run downhill against the wind, beating its way through the rocks, crossing the steppes, the meadows. The river changed its bed, leaving it dried by the sun, and in a barely visible watery thread made its way along the rocks, faithful to its eternal duty. It was a stream that had lost hope for help from heaven—a saving rain, but with the first rain, the water changed its shores, broke rocks, cast huge trees in the air and rushed madly down that same eternal road. . . .

Sententious! I couldn't believe myself and was afraid when I went to sleep that I would forget the word that had newly returned to me. But the word didn't disappear.

For a week I didn't understand what the word meant. I whispered it, amused and frightened my neighbors with it. I wanted an explanation, a definition, a translation. . . .

Many days passed before I learned to call forth from the depth of memory new words, one after the other. Each came with difficulty; each appeared suddenly and separately. Thoughts and words didn't return in streams. Each returned alone, unaccompanied by the watchful guards of familiar words. Each appeared first on the tongue and only later in the mind.

And then came the day when everyone, all fifty workers, dropped their work and ran to the village, to the river, climbing out of their ditches, abandoning half-sawn-through trees and the uncooked soup in the pot. They all ran quicker than me, but I hobbled up in time, aiding myself in this downhill run with my hands.

The chief had arrived from Magadan. The day was clear, hot, dry. On an enormous fir stump stood a record player. Overcoming the hiss of the needle, it was playing symphonic music.

And everyone stood around—murderers and horse thieves, common criminals and political prisoners, foremen and workers. And the chief stood there too. And the expression on his face was such that he seemed to have written the music for us, for our desolate sojourn in the taiga. The shellacked record spun and hissed, and the stump itself, wound up in three hundred circles over the past three hundred years, spun like a taut spring. . . .

PART THREE

DEFIANCE

Prosthetic Appliances

>>>

THE CAMP'S solitary confinement block was old, old. It seemed
that all you had to do was to kick one of the wooden walls and
its logs would collapse, disintegrate. But the block did not collapse and all seven cells did faithful service. Of course, any
loudly spoken word could be heard by one's neighbors, but the
inmates of the block were afraid of punishment. If the guard
on duty marked the cell with a chalk X, the cell was deprived
of hot food. Two Xs meant no bread as well. The block was
used for camp offenses; anyone suspected of something more
dangerous was taken away to Central Control.

For the first time all the prisoners entrusted with administrative work had suddenly been arrested. Some major affair,
some camp trial was being put together. By someone's command.

Now all six of us were standing in the narrow corridor,
surrounded by guards, feeling and understanding only one
thing: that we had been caught by the teeth of that same
machine as several years before and that we would learn the
reason only tomorrow, no earlier.

We were all made to undress to our underwear and were
led into a separate cell. The storekeeper recorded things taken
for storage, stuffed them into sacks, attached tags, wrote. I
knew the name of the investigator supervising the "operation"—Pesniakevich.

The first man was on crutches. He sat down on a bench
next to the lamp, put the crutches on the floor, and began to
undress. He was wearing a steel corset.

"Should I take it off?"

"Of course."

The man began to unlace the cords of the corset and the investigator Pesniakevich bent down to help him.

"Do you recognize me, old friend?" The question was asked in thieves' slang, in a confidential manner.

"I recognize you, Pleve."

The man in the corset was Pleve, supervisor of the camp tailor shop. It was an important job involving twenty tailors who, with the permission of the administration, filled individual orders even from outside the camp.

The naked man turned over on the bench. On the floor lay the steel corset as the report of confiscated items was composed.

"What's this thing called?" asked the block storekeeper, touching the corset with the toe of his boot.

"A steel prosthetic corset," answered the naked man.

Pesniakevich went off to the side and I asked Pleve how he knew him.

"His mother kept a whorehouse in Minsk before the Revolution. I used to go there," Pleve answered coldly.

Pesniakevich emerged from the depths of the corridor with four guards. They picked Pleve up by his arms and legs and carried him into the cell. The lock snapped shut.

Next was Karavaev, manager of the stable. A former soldier of the famous Budyony Brigade, he had lost an arm in the Civil War.

Karavaev banged on the officer of the guards' table with the steel of his artificial limb.

"You bastards."

"Drop the metal. Let's have the arm."

Karavaev raised the untied limb, but the guards jumped the cavalryman and shoved him into the cell. There ensued a flood of elaborate obscenities.

"Listen, Karavaev," said the chief guard of the block. "We'll take away your hot food if you make noise."

"To hell with your hot food."

The head guard took a piece of chalk out of his pocket and made an X on Karavaev's cell.

"Who's going to sign for the arm?"

"No one. Put a check mark," commanded Pesniakevich.

Now it was the turn of our doctor, Zhitkov. A deaf old man, he wore a hearing aid. After him was Colonel Panin, manager of the carpentry shop. A shell had taken off the colonel's leg somewhere in East Prussia during the First World War. He was an excellent carpenter, and he explained to me that before the Revolution children of the nobility were often taught some hand trade. The old man unsnapped his prosthetic leg and hopped into his cell on one leg.

There were only two of us left—Shor, Grisha Shor the senior brigade leader, and myself.

"Look how cleverly things are going," Grisha said; the nervous mirth of the arrest was overtaking him. "One turns in a leg; another an arm; I'll give an eye." Adroitly he plucked out his porcelain right eye and showed it to me in his palm.

"You have an artificial eye?" I said in amazement. "I never noticed."

"You are not very observant. But then the eye is a good match."

While Grisha's eye was being recorded, the chief guard couldn't control himself and started giggling.

"That one gives us his arm; this one turns in his leg; another gives his back, and this one gives his eye. We'll have all the parts of the body at this rate. How about you?" He looked over my naked body carefully.

"What will you give up? Your soul?"

"No," I said. "You can't have my soul."

Quiet

>>

ALL OF US, the whole work gang, took our places in the camp dining hall with a mixture of surprise, suspicion, caution, and fear. The tables were the same dirty, sticky ones we had eaten at since we had arrived. The tables should not have been sticky because the last thing anyone wanted was to spill his soup. But there were no spoons, and any spilled soup was scraped together by fingers and simply licked up.

It was dinnertime for the night shift. Our work gang was hidden away among the night shift so that no one might see us—as if there were anyone to see us! We were the weakest, the worst, the hungriest. We were the human trash, but they had to feed us, and not with garbage or leftovers. We too had to receive a certain amount of fats, solid foods, and mainly bread—bread that was just the same as that given to the best work gangs that still preserved their strength and were fulfilling the plan of "basic production": gold, gold, gold . . .

When we were fed, it was always last. Night or day, it didn't make any difference. Tonight we were last again.

We lived in a section of the barracks. I knew some of the semicorpses, either from prison or from transit camps. I moved together with these lumps in peacoats, cloth hats that covered the ears and were not taken off except for visits to the bathhouse, quilted jackets made from torn pants that had been singed at campfires. Only by memory did I recognize the redfaced Tartar, Mutalov, who had been the only resident in all Chikment whose two-storied house had an iron roof, and Efremov, the former first secretary of the Chikment City Council, who had liquidated Mulatov as a class in 1930.

There too was Oxman, former head of a divisional propaganda office until Marshal Timoshenko, who was not yet a marshal, kicked him out of the division as a Jew. Also there was Lupinov, assistant to the supreme prosecutor of the USSR, Vyshinsky. Zhavoronkov was a train engineer for the Savelisk Depo. Also there was the former head of the secret police in the city of Gorky who had had a quarrel with one of his former "wards" when they met at a transit camp:

"So they beat you? So what? You signed, so you're an enemy. You interfere with the Soviet government, keep us from working. It's because of insects like you that I got fifteen years."

I couldn't help butting in: "Listening to you, I don't know whether to laugh or spit in your face. . . ."

There were various people in this doomed brigade. There was a member of the religious sect, "God Knows." Maybe the sect had a different name, but that was the one invariable answer the man ever gave in response to questions from the guards.

I remember, of course, the sectarian's name—Dmitriev—although he never answered to it. Dmitriev was moved, placed in line, led by his companions or the work gang leader.

The convoy changed frequently, and almost every new commander tried to find out why he refused to respond to the loud command—"Names!"—shouted out before the men set out for work.

The work gang leader would briefly explain the "circumstances," and the relieved guard would continue the roll call.

The sectarian got on everyone's nerves in the barracks. At night we couldn't sleep because of the cold and warmed ourselves at the iron stove, wrapping our arms around it and gathering the departing warmth of cooling iron, pressing our faces to the metal.

Naturally we blocked this feeble warmth from the other residents of the barracks who, hungry too, couldn't sleep in their distant corners covered with frost. From those corners someone with the right to shout or even beat us would jump out and drive the hungry workers from the stove with oaths and kicks.

You could stand at the stove and legally dry your bread, but who had bread to dry? And how many hours could you take to dry a piece of bread?

We hated the administration and the camp guards, hated each other, and most of all we hated the sectarian—for his songs, hymns, psalms . . .

Silently we clutched the stove. The sectarian sang in a

hoarse voice as if he had a cold. He sang softly, but his hymns and psalms were endless.

The sectarian and I worked as a pair. The other members of the section rested from the singing while working, but I didn't have even that relief.

"Shut up!" someone shouted at the sectarian.

"I would have died long ago if it weren't for singing these songs. I want to go away—into the frost. But I'm too weak. If I were just a little stronger. I don't ask God for death. He sees everything himself."

There were other people in the brigade, wrapped in rags, just as dirty and hungry, with the same gleam in their eyes. Who were they? Generals? Heroes of the Spanish War? Russian writers? Collective farm workers from Volokolamsk?

We sat in the dining hall wondering why we weren't being fed, whom they were waiting for. What news was to be announced? For us any news could only be good. There is a certain point beyond which anything is an improvement. The news could only be good. Everyone understood that—not with their minds, but with their bodies.

The door of the serving window opened from inside and we were brought soup in bowls—hot! Kasha—warm! And cranberry pudding for dessert—almost cold! Everyone was given a spoon, and the head of the brigade warned us that we would have to return the spoons. Of course we would return the spoons. Why did we need spoons? To exchange for tobacco in other barracks? Of course we'll return the spoons. Why do we need spoons? We're used to eating straight from the bowl. Who needs a spoon? Anything that's left in the bottom of the bowl can be pushed with fingers to the edge . . .

There was no need to think; in front of us was food. They gave us bread—two hundred grams. "You get only one ration of bread," the brigade leader declared with a note of excited solemnity, "but you can eat your fill of the rest."

And we ate "our fill." Any soup consists of two parts: the thick part and the liquid. We got "our fill" of the liquid. But of the kasha we got as much as we wanted. Dessert was lukewarm water with a light taste of starch and a trace of dissolved sugar. This was the cranberry pudding.

A convict's stomach is not rendered insensitive by hunger and the coarse food. On the contrary, its sensitivity to taste is heightened. The qualitative reaction of a convict's stomach is in no way inferior to that of the finest laboratory. No "free" stomach could have discovered the presence of sugar in the pudding that we ate or, rather, drank that night in Kolyma at the "Partisan Mine," but the pudding seemed sweet, exquisitely sweet. It seemed a miracle and everyone remembered that sugar still existed in the world and that it even ended up in the convict's pot. What magician ? . .

The magician was not far away. We looked him over after the second dish of the second dinner.

"Just one ration of bread," said the brigade leader. "Eat your fill of the rest." He looked at the magician.

"Yes, of course," said the magician.

He was a small clean brunette whose face had not yet suffered from frostbite.

Our superiors, supervisors, overseers, camp administrators, guards had all been to Kolyma, and Siberia had signed its name on each of their faces, left its mark, cut extra wrinkles, and put the mark of frostbite as an indelible brand!

On the rosy face of the clean dark-haired little man there was still no spot, no brand. This was the new senior "educator" of our camp, and he had just arrived from the continent. The "senior educator" was conducting an experiment.

The "educator" insisted to the head of the camp that an ancient Kolyma custom be abolished: traditionally the remains of the soup and kasha had been carried daily from the kitchen to the criminal barracks when only the thick part was left on the bottom. This had always been given out to the best work gangs to support not the hungriest, but the least hungry work gangs, to encourage them to fulfill the "plan" and turn everything into gold—even the souls and bodies of the administration, the guards, the convicts.

Those work gangs as well as the criminal element had

become accustomed to these leftovers, but the new "educator" was not in agreement with the custom and insisted that the leftovers be given to the weakest, the hungriest to "waken their conscience."

"They're so hardened, they have no conscience," the foreman attempted to intervene, but the "educator" was firm and received permission to try the experiment.

Our brigade, the hungriest, was chosen for the experiment.

"Now you'll see. A man will eat and in gratitude work better for the state. How can you expect any work out of these 'goners'? 'Goners' is the right word, isn't it? That's the first word of local convict slang I learned here in Kolyma. Am I saying it right?"

"Yeah," said the area chief, an old resident of Kolyma and not a convict. He'd "plowed under" thousands at this mine and had come especially to enjoy the experiment.

"You could feed these loafers and fakers meat and chocolate for a month with no work, and even then they wouldn't work. Something must have changed in their skulls. They're culls, rejects. Production demands that we feed the ones that work and not these loafers!"

Standing there beside the serving window, they began to quarrel and shout. The "educator" was vehemently making some point. The area chief was listening with a displeased expression, and when the name Makarenko was mentioned, he threw up his hands and walked away.

We each prayed to our own god, the sectarian to his own. We prayed that the window would not be closed and that the educator would win out. The collective convict will of twenty men strained itself . . . and the "educator" had his way.

Not wanting to part with a miracle, we kept on eating.

The area chief took out his watch, but the horn was already sounding—a shrill camp siren calling us to work.

"Okay, you busy bees," said the new educator, uncertainly enunciating his unnecessary phrase. "I've done everything I could. I did it for you. Now it's up to you to answer by working, and only by working."

"We'll work, citizen chief," pronounced the former head of the Supreme Soviet of the USSR with dignity, tying his peacoat shut with a dirty towel and blowing warm air into his mittens.

The door opened and in a cloud of white steam we all came out into the frost to remember this success for the rest of our lives—that is, those who had lives left to live. The frost didn't seem so bad to us—but only at first. It was too cold to be ignored.

We came to the mine, sat down in a circle to wait for the work gang leader at the very spot where we used to have a fire, breathe into the gold flame, where we singed our mittens, caps, pants, peacoats, jackets, vainly attempting to get warm and escape the cold. But the fire was a long time ago—the previous year, perhaps. This winter the workers were not permitted to warm themselves; only the guard had permission. He sat down, rearranged the burning logs, and the fire blazed higher. Then he buttoned his sheepskin coat, sat on a log, and stood his rifle beside him.

A white fog surrounded the mine, which was lit only by the fire of the guard. The sectarian, who was sitting next to me, stood up and walked past the guard into the fog, into the sky. . . .

"Halt! Halt!"

The guard wasn't a bad sort, but he knew his rifle well.

"Halt!"

A shot rang out, then the dry sound of a gun being cocked. The sectarian didn't disappear into the fog, and there was a second shot. . . .

"See, sucker?" said the area chief to the educator, taking his phrase from the criminal world. They had come to the mine, and the educator did not dare show surprise at the murder, and the area chief didn't know how to.

"There's your experiment for you. These bastards are

working worse than before. An extra dinner just gives them extra strength to fight the cold. Remember this: only the cold will squeeze work out of them. Not your dinner and not a punch in the ear from me—only the cold. They wave their hands to get warm. But we put picks and shovels into these hands. What's the difference what they wave? We set wheel-barrows, boxes, sledges in front of them, and the mine fulfills the plan. Puts out gold . . .

"Now they're full and won't work at all. Not until they get cold. Then they'll start moving those shovels. But feeding them is useless. You sure made yourself look like an idiot civil-ian with that dinner. But we can forgive it the first time. We were all suckers like that at first."

"I had no idea they were such slime," said the educator.

"Next time you'll believe those of us who have experi-ence. We shot one today. A loafer. Ate his government ration six months for nothing. Say it: 'loafer.' "

"Loafer," repeated the educator.

I was standing next to them but they saw no need to let that bother them. I had a legitimate reason for waiting: the work gang leader was supposed to bring me a new partner. He brought Lupilov, the former assistant to the Soviet prosecutor general. The two of us started tossing dynamited rock into large boxes. It was the same work that the sectarian and I used to do.

Later we returned along the same road, as usual not hav-ing met our quota, but not caring about it either. But somehow it didn't seem as cold as usual.

We tried to work, but our lives were too distant from any-thing that could be expressed in figures, wheelbarrows, or per-cent of plan. The figures were a mockery. But for an hour, for one moment after that night's dinner, we got our strength back.

And suddenly I realized that that night's dinner had given the sectarian the strength he needed for his suicide. He needed that extra portion of kasha to make up his mind to die.

There are times when a man has to hurry so as not to lose his will to die.

As usual, we encircled the stove. But today there was no one to sing any hymns. And I guess I was even happy that it was finally quiet.

Major Pugachov's Last Battle

>>

A LOT OF TIME must have passed between the beginning and end of these events, for the human experience acquired in the far north is so great that months are considered equivalent to years. Even the state recognizes this by increasing salaries and fringe benefits to workers of the north. It is a land of hopes and therefore of rumors, guesses, suppositions, and hypothesizing. In the north any event is encrusted with rumor more quickly than a local official's emergency report about it can reach the "higher spheres."

It was rumored that when a party boss on an inspection tour described the camp's cultural activities as lame on both feet, the "activities director," Major Pugachov, said to the guest:

"Don't let that bother you, sir, we're preparing a concert that all Kolyma will talk about."

We could begin the story straightaway with the report of Braude, a surgeon sent by the central hospital to the region of military activities. We could begin with the letter of Yashka Kushen, a convict orderly who was a patient in the hospital. Kuchen wrote the letter with his left hand, since his right shoulder had been shot clean through by a rifle bullet.

Or we could begin with the story of Dr. Potalina who saw nothing, heard nothing, and was gone when all the unusual events took place. It was precisely her absence that the prosecutor classified as a "false alibi," criminal inaction, or whatever the term may be in a legal jargon.

The arrests of the thirties were arrests of random victims of the false and terrifying theory of a heightened class struggle accompanying the strengthening of socialism. The professors, union officials, soldiers, and workers who filled the prisons to overflowing at that period had nothing to defend themselves with except, perhaps, personal honesty and naiveté—precisely those qualities that lightened rather than hindered the punitive work of "justice" of the day. The absence of any unifying idea undermined the moral resistance of the prisoners to an unusual degree. They were neither enemies of the government nor state criminals, and they died, not even understanding why they had to die. Their self-esteem and bitterness had no point of support. Separated, they perished in the white Kolyma desert from hunger, cold, work, beatings, and diseases. They immediately learned not to defend or support each other. This was precisely the goal of the authorities. The souls of those who remained alive were utterly corrupted, and their bodies did not possess the qualities necessary for physical labor.

After the war, ship after ship delivered their replacements—former Soviet citizens who were "repatriated" directly to the far northeast.

Among them were many people with different experiences and habits acquired during the war, courageous people who knew how to take chances and who believed only in the gun. There were officers and soldiers, fliers and scouts. . . .

Accustomed to the angelic patience and slavish submissiveness of the "Trotskyites," the camp administration was not in the least concerned and expected nothing new.

New arrivals asked the surviving "aborigines":

"Why do you eat your soup and kasha in the dining hall, but take your bread with you back to the barracks? Why can't you eat the bread with your soup the way the rest of the world does?"

Smiling with the cracks of their blue mouths and showing their gums, toothless from scurvy, the local residents would answer the naïve newcomers:

"In two weeks each of you will understand, and each of you will do the same."

How could they be told that they had never in their lives known true hunger, hunger that lasts for years and breaks the will? How could anyone explain the passionate, all-engulfing desire to prolong the process of eating, the supreme bliss of washing down one's bread ration with a mug of tasteless, but hot melted snow in the barracks?

But not all of the newcomers shook their heads in contempt and walked away.

Major Pugachov clearly realized that they had been delivered to their deaths—to replace these living corpses. They had been brought in the fall. With winter coming on, there was no place to run to, but in the summer a man could at least die free even if he couldn't hope to escape completely.

It was virtually the only conspiracy in twenty years, and its web was spun all winter.

Pugachov realized that only those who did not work in the mine's general work gang could survive the winter and still be capable of an escape attempt. After a few weeks in the work gang no one would run anywhere.

Slowly, one by one, the participants of the conspiracy became trusties. Soldatov became a cook, and Pugachov himself was appointed activities director. There were two work gang leaders, a paramedic and Ivashenko, who had formerly been a mechanic and now repaired weapons for the guards.

But no one was permitted outside "the wire" without guards.

The blinding Kolyma spring began—without a single rain, without any movement of ice on the rivers, without the singing of any bird. Little by little, the sun melted the snow, leaving it only in those crevices where warm rays couldn't pierce. In the canyons and ravines, the snow lay like silver bullion till the next year.

And the designated day arrived.

There was a knock at the door of the guard hut next to the camp gates where one door led in and the other out of the camp. The guard on duty yawned and glanced at the clock. It was 5:00 A.M. "Just five," he thought.

The guard threw back the latch and admitted the man who had knocked. It was the camp cook, the convict Gorbunov. He'd come for the keys to the food storeroom. The keys were kept in the guardhouse, and Gorbunov came for them three times a day. He returned them later.

The guard on duty was supposed to open the kitchen cupboard, but he knew it was hopeless to try to control the cook, that no locks would help if the cook wanted to steal, so he entrusted the keys to the cook—especially at five in the morning.

The guard had worked more than ten years in Kolyma, had been receiving a double salary for a long time, and had given the keys to the cooks thousands of times.

"Take 'em," he muttered and reached for the ruler to write up the morning report.

Gorbunov walked behind the guard, took the keys from the nail, put them in his pocket, and grabbed the guard from behind by the neck. At that very moment the door opened and the mechanic, Ivashenko, came through the door leading into the camp.

Ivashenko helped Gorbunov strangle the guard and drag his body behind the cabinet. Ivashenko stuck the guard's revolver into his own pocket. Through the window that faced outward they could see a second guard returning along the path. Hurriedly Ivashenko donned the coat and cap of the dead man, snapped the belt shut, and sat down at the table as if he were the guard. The second guard opened the door and strode into the dark hovel of the guardhouse. He was immediately seized, strangled, and thrown behind the cabinet.

Gorbunov put on the guard's clothing; the two conspirators now had uniforms and weapons. Everything was proceeding according to Major Pugachov's schedule. Suddenly the wife of the second guard appeared. She'd come for the keys that her husband had accidently taken with him.

"We won't strangle the woman," said Gorbunov, and she was tied, gagged with a towel, and put in the corner.

One of the work gangs returned from work. This had been foreseen. The overseer who entered the guardhouse was immediately disarmed and bound by the two "guards." His rifle was now in the hands of the escapees. From that moment Major Pugachov took command of the operation.

The area before the gates was open to fire from two guard towers. The sentries noticed nothing unusual.

A work gang was formed somewhat earlier than usual, but in the north who can say what is early and what is late? It seemed early, but maybe it was late.

The work gang of ten men moved down the road to the mine, two by two in column. In the front and in the rear, six meters from the column of prisoners as required by the instructions, were two overcoated guards. One of them held a rifle.

From the guard tower the sentry noticed that the group turned from the road onto the path that led past the buildings where all sixty of the guards were quartered.

The sleeping quarters of the guards ware located in the far end of the building. Just before the door stood the guard hut of the man on duty, and pyramids of rifles. Drowsing by the window the guard noticed, in a half sleep, that one of the other guards was leading a gang of prisoners down the path past the windows of the guard quarters.

"That must be Chernenko," the duty officer thought. "I must remember to write a report on him."

The duty officer was grand master of petty squabbles, and he never missed a legitimate opportunity to play a dirty trick on someone.

This was his last thought. The door flew open and three soldiers came running into the barracks. Two rushed to the doors of the sleeping quarters and the third shot the duty

officer point-blank. The soldiers were followed by the prisoners, who rushed to the pyramid of weapons; in their hands
were rifles and machine guns. Major Pugachov threw open
the door to the sleeping quarters. The soldiers, barefoot and
still in their underwear, rushed to the door, but two machine-
gun bursts at the ceiling stopped them.

"Lie down," Pugachov ordered, and the soldiers crawled
under their cots. The machine gunners remained on guard beside the door.

The "work gang" changed unhurriedly into military uniform and began gathering up food, weapons, and ammunition.

Pugachov ordered them not to take any food except biscuits and chocolate. In return they took as many weapons and
as much ammunition as possible.

The paramedic hung the first-aid bag over his shoulder.

Once again the escapees felt they were soldiers.

Before them was the taiga, but was it any more terrible
than the marshes of Stokhod?

They walked out onto the highway, and Pugachov raised
his hand to stop a passing truck.

"Get out!" He opened the door of the driver's cab.

"But I . . ."

"Climb out, I tell you."

The driver got out, and Georgadze, lieutenant of the tank
troops, got behind the wheel. Beside him was Pugachov. The
escapee soldiers crawled into the back, and the truck sped off.

"There ought to be a right turn about here."

"We're out of gas!"

Pugachov cursed.

They entered the taiga as if they were diving into water,
disappearing immediately in the enormous silent forest.
Checking the map, they remained on the cherished path to
freedom, pushing their way straight through the amazing
local underbrush.

Camp was set up quickly for the night, as if they were
used to doing it.

Only Ashot and Malinin couldn't manage to quiet down.

"What's the problem over there?" asked Pugachov.

"Ashot keeps trying to prove that Adam was deported from paradise to Ceylon."

"Why Ceylon?"

"That's what the Muslims say," responded Ashot.

"Are you a Tartar?"

"Not me, my wife is."

"I never heard anything of the sort," said Pugachov, smiling.

"Right, and neither did I," Malinin joined in.

"All right, knock it off. Let's get some sleep."

It was cold and Major Pugachov woke up. Soldatov was sitting up, alert, holding the machine gun on his knees. Pugachov lay on his back and located the North Star, the favorite star of all wanderers. The constellations here were arranged differently than in European Russia; the map of the firmament was slightly shifted, and the Big Dipper had slid down to the horizon. The taiga was cold and stern, and the enormous twisted pines stood far from each other. The forest was filled with the anxious silence familiar to all hunters. This time Pugachov was not the hunter, but a tracked beast, and the forest silence was thrice dangerous.

It was his first night of liberty, the first night after long months and years of torment. Lying on his back, he recalled how everything before him had begun as if it were a detective film. It was as if Pugachov were playing back a film of his twelve comrades so that the lazy everyday course of events flashed by with unbelievable speed. And now they had finished the film and were staring at the inscription, "THE END." They were free, but this was only the beginning of the struggle, the game, of life. . . .

Major Pugachov remembered the German prisoner-of-war camp from which he had escaped in 1944. The front was nearing the town, and he was working as a truck driver on cleanup details inside the enormous camp. He recalled how he had driven through the single strand of barbed wire at high speed, ripping up the wooden posts that had been hurriedly punched into the ground. He remembered the sentry shots, shouting, the mad, zigzag drive through the town, the abandoned truck, the night road to the front and the meetings with his army, the interrogation, the accusation of espionage, and the sentence—twenty-five years.

Major Pugachov remembered how Vlasov's emissaries had come to the camp with a "manifesto" to the hungry, tormented Russian soldiers.

"Your government has long since renounced you. Any prisoner of war is a traitor in the eyes of your government," the Vlasovites said. And they showed Moscow newspapers with their orders and speeches. The prisoners of war had already heard of this earlier. It was no accident that Russian prisoners of war were the only ones not to receive packages. Frenchmen, Americans, Englishmen, and prisoners of all nations received packages, letters, had their own national clubs, and enjoyed each other's friendship. The Russians had nothing except hunger and bitterness for the entire world. It was no wonder that so many men from the German prisoner-of-war camps joined the "Russian Army of Liberation."

Major Pugachov did not believe Vlasov's officers until he made his way back to the Red Army. Everything that the Vlasovites had said was true. The government had no use for him. The government was afraid of him. Later came the cattle cars with bars on the windows and guards, the long trip to Eastern Siberia, the sea, the ship's hold, and the gold mines of the far north. And the hungry winter.

Pugachov sat up, and Soldatov gestured to him with his hand. It was Soldatov who had the honor of beginning the entire affair, although he was among the last to be accepted into the conspiracy. Soldatov had not lost his courage, panicked, or betrayed anyone. A good man!

At his feet lay Captain Khrustalyov, a flier whose fate was similar to Pugachov's: his plane shot down by the Germans, captivity, hunger, escape, and a military tribunal and the forced-labor camp. Khrustalyov had just turned over on his other side, and his cheek was red from where he had been lying on it. It was Khrustalyov whom Pugachov had first chosen several months before to reveal his plan. They agreed it was better to die than be a convict, better to die with a gun in hand than be exhausted by hunger, rifle butts, and the boots of the guards.

Both Khrustalyov and the major were men of action, and they discussed in minute detail the insignificant chance for which these twelve men were risking their lives. The plan was to hijack a plane from the airport. There were several airports in the vicinity, and the men were on their way through the taiga to the nearest one. Khrustalyov was the group leader whom the escapees sent for after attacking the guards. Pugachov didn't want to leave without his closest friend. Now Khrustalyov was sleeping quietly and soundly.

Next to him lay Ivashenko, the mechanic who repaired the guards' weapons. Ivashenko had learned everything they needed to know for a successful operation: where the weapons were kept, who was on duty, where the munitions stores were. Ivashenko had been a military intelligence officer.

Levitsky and Ignatovich, pilots and friends of Captain Khrustalyov, lay pressed against each other.

The tankman, Polyakov, had spread his hands on the backs of his neighbors, the huge Georgadze and the bald joker Ashot, whose surname the major couldn't remember at the moment. Head resting on his first-aid bag, Sasha Malinin was sound asleep. He'd started out as a paramedic—first in the army, then in the camps, then under Pugachov's command.

Pugachov smiled. Each had surely imagined the escape in his own way, but Pugachov could see that everything was going smoothly and each understood the other perfectly. Pugachov was convinced he had done the right thing. Each knew that events were developing as they should. There was a commander, there was a goal—a confident commander and a difficult goal. There were weapons and freedom. They slept a sound soldier's sleep even in this empty pale-lilac polar night with its strange but beautiful light in which the trees cast no shadows.

He had promised them freedom, and they had received freedom. He led them to their deaths, and they didn't fear death.

"No one betrayed us," thought Pugachov, "right up to the very last day." Many people in the camp had known of the planned escape. Selection of participants had taken several months, and Pugachov had spoken openly to many who refused, but no one had turned them in. This knowledge reconciled Pugachov with life.

"They're good men," he whispered and smiled.

They ate some biscuits and chocolate and went on in silence, led by the almost indistinguishable path.

"It's a bear path," said Soldatov who had hunted in Siberia.

Pugachov and Khrustalyov climbed up to the pass to a cartographic tripod and used the telescope to look down to the gray stripes of the river and highway. The river was like any other river, but the highway was filled with trucks and people for tens of miles.

"Must be convicts," suggested Khrustalyov.

Pugachov examined them carefully.

"No, they're soldiers looking for us. We'll have to split up," said Pugachov. "Eight men can sleep in the haystacks, and the four of us will check out that ravine. We'll return by morning if everything looks all right."

They passed through a small grove of trees to the riverbed. They had to run back.

"Look, there are too many of them. We'll have to go back up the river."

Breathing heavily, they quickly climbed back up the riverbed, inadvertently dislodging loose rocks that roared down right to the feet of the attackers.

Levitsky turned, fired, and fell. A bullet had caught him square in the eye.

Georgadze stopped beside a large rock, turned, and stopped the soldiers coming after them with a machine-gun burst. But it was not for long; his machine gun jammed, and only the rifle was still functioning.

"Go on alone," said Khrustalyov to the major. "I'll cover you." He aimed methodically, shooting at anyone who showed himself. Khrustalyov caught up with them, shouting: "They're coming." He fell, and people began running out from behind the large rock.

Pugachov rushed forward, fired at the attackers, and leaped down from the pass's plateau into the narrow river-bed. The stones he knocked loose as he fell roared down the slope.

He ran through the roadless taiga until his strength failed.

Above the forest meadow the sun rose, and the people hiding in haystacks could easily make out figures of men in military uniforms on all sides of the meadow.

"I guess this is the end?" Ivashenko said, and nudged Khachaturian with his elbow.

"Why the end?" Ashot said as he aimed. The rifle shot rang out, and a soldier fell on the path.

At a command the soldiers rushed the swamp and hay-stacks. Shots cracked and groans were heard.

The attack was repulsed. Several wounded men lay among the clumps of marsh grass.

"Medic, crawl over there," an officer ordered. They'd shown foresight and brought along Yasha Kushen, a former resident of West Byelorussia, now a convict paramedic. Without saying a word, convict Kushen crawled over to the wounded man, waving his first-aid bag. The bullet that struck Kushen in the shoulder stopped him halfway.

The head of the guard detail that the escapees had just disarmed jumped up without any sign of fear and shouted:

"Hey, Ivashenko, Soldatov, Pugachov. Give up, you're surrounded. There's no way out!"

"Okay, come and get the weapons, shouted Ivashenko from behind the haystack.

And Bobylyov, head of the guards, ran splashing through the marsh toward the haystacks.

He had covered half the way when Ivashenko's shot cracked out. The bullet caught Bobylyov directly in the forehead.

"Good boy," Soldatov praised his comrade. "The chief was so brave because they would have either shot him for our escape or given him a sentence in the camps. Hold your ground!"

They were shooting from all directions. Machine guns began to crackle.

Soldatov felt a burning sensation in both legs, and the head of the dead Ivashenko fell on his shoulder.

Another haystack fell silent. A dozen bodies lay in the marsh.

Soldatov kept on shooting until something struck him in the head and he lost consciousness.

Nikolay Braude, chief surgeon of the main hospital, was summoned by Major General Artemyev, one of four Kolyma generals and chief of the whole Kolyma camp. Braude was sent to the village of Lichan together with "two paramedics, bandages, and surgical instruments." That was how the order read.

Braude didn't try to guess what might have happened and quickly set out as directed in a beat-up one-and-a-half-ton hospital truck. Powerful Studebakers loaded with armed soldiers streamed past the hospital truck on the highway. It was only about twenty miles, but because of frequent stops caused by heavy traffic and roadblocks to check documents, it took Braude three hours to reach the area.

Major General Artemyev was waiting for the surgeon in the apartment of the local camp head. Both Braude and Artemyev were long-term residents of Kolyma and fate had brought them together a number of times in the past.

"What's up, a war?" Braude asked the general when they met.

"I don't know if you'd call it a war, but there were twenty-eight dead in the first battle. You'll see the wounded yourself."

While Braude washed his hands in a basin hanging on the door, the general told him of the escape.

"And you called for planes, I suppose? A couple of squadrons, a few bombs here and there . . . Or maybe you opted for an atom bomb?"

"That's right, make a joke of it," said the general. "I tell you I'm not joking when I say that I'm waiting for my orders. I'll be lucky if I just lose my job. They could even try me. Things like that have happened before."

Yes, Braude knew that things like that had happened before. Several years earlier three thousand people were sent on foot in winter to one of the ports, but supplies stored on shore were destroyed by a storm while the group was underway. Of three thousand, only three hundred people remained alive. The second-in-command in the camp administration who had signed the orders to send the group was made a scapegoat and tried.

Braude and his paramedics worked until evening, removing bullets, amputating, bandaging. Only soldiers of the guard were among the wounded; there were no escapees.

The next day toward evening more wounded were brought in. Surrounded by officers of the guard, two soldiers carried in the first and only escapee whom Braude was to see. The escapee was in military uniform and differed from the soldiers only in that he was unshaven. Both shinbones and his left shoulder were broken by bullets, and there was a head wound with damage to the parietal bone. The man was unconscious.

Braude rendered him first aid and, as Artemyev had ordered, the wounded man and his guards were taken to the central hospital where there were the necessary facilities for a serious operation.

It was all over. Nearby stood an army truck covered with a tarpaulin. It contained the bodies of the dead escapees. Next to it was a second truck with the bodies of the dead soldiers.

But Major Pugachov was crawling down the edge of the ravine.

They could have sent the army home after this victory, but trucks with soldiers continued to travel along the thousand-mile highway for many days.

They couldn't find the twelfth man—Major Pugachov.

Soldatov took a long time to recover—to be shot. But then that was the only death sentence out of sixty. Such was the number of friends and acquaintances who were sent before the military tribunal. The head of the local camp was sentenced to ten years. The head of the medical section, Dr. Potalina, was acquitted, and she changed her place of employment almost as soon as the trial was over. Major General Artemyev's words were prophetic: he was removed from his position in the guard.

Pugachov dragged himself into the narrow throat of the cave. It was a bear's den, the beast's winter quarters, and the animal had long since left to wander the taiga. Bear hairs could still be seen on the cave walls and stone floor.

"How quickly it's all ended," thought Pugachov. "They'll bring dogs and find me."

Lying in the cave, he remembered his difficult male life, a life that was to end on a bear path in the taiga. He remembered people—all of whom he had respected and loved, beginning with his mother. He remembered his schoolteacher, Maria Ivanovna, and her quilted jacket of threadbare black velvet that was turning red. There were many, many others with whom fate had thrown him together.

But better than all, more noble than all were his eleven dead comrades. None of the other people in his life had endured such disappointments, deceit, lies. And in this northern hell they had found within themselves the strength to believe in him, Pugachov, and to stretch out their hands to freedom. These men who had died in battle were the best men he had known in his life.

Pugachov picked a blueberry from a shrub that grew at the entrance to the cave. Last year's wrinkled fruit burst in his fingers, and he licked them clean. The overripe fruit was as tasteless as snow water. The skin of the berry stuck to his dry tongue.

Yes, they were the best. He remembered Ashot's surname now; it was Khachaturian.

Major Pugachov remembered each of them, one after the other, and smiled at each. Then he put the muzzle of the pistol in his mouth and for the last time in his life fired a shot.

PART FOUR

THE CRIMINAL
WORLD

On Tick

>>

THEY WERE PLAYING CARDS on Naumov's berth in the barracks for the mine's horse drivers. The overseer on duty
never looked into that barracks, since he considered that his
main duty was to keep an eye on prisoners convicted according to Article 58 of the Criminal Code—political prisoners. In a
word, the horse drivers' barracks was the safest place to be,
and every night the criminal element in the camp gathered
there to play cards.

In a corner of the barracks on the lower cots quilts of
various colors were spread. To the corner post was wired a
burning *kolymka*—a homemade lamp that worked on gas
fumes. Three or four open-ended copper tubes were soldered
to the lid of a tin can. It was a very simple device. When hot
coals were placed on the lid, the gas heated up and fumes rose
along the pipes, burning at the pipe ends when lit by a match.

On the blankets lay a dirty feather pillow and on either
side of it the players sat, their legs tucked under them. A new
deck of cards lay on the pillow. These were not ordinary cards,
but a homemade prison deck made with amazing deftness by
the local wizards. They needed only paper, a piece of bread
(chewed and pressed through a rag, it produced starch to glue
the sheets together), an indelible pencil stub, and a knife (to
cut stencils for the card suits and the cards themselves).

Today's cards were cut from a book by Victor Hugo; someone had forgotten the book the day before in the office. It had
heavy thick paper, so there was no need to glue sheets
together.

A dirty hand with the slender white fingers of a nonwork-
ing man was patting the deck on the pillow. The nail of the

little finger was of unusual length—a fashion among the criminals just like their gold, that is, bronze crowns put on completely healthy teeth. As for the fingernails, nail polish would
unquestionably have become popular in the "criminal world"
if it were possible to obtain polish in prison circumstances.

The owner of the deck was running his left hand through
his sticky, dirty, light-colored hair which was meticulously cut
with a square back. Everything in his face—the low unwrin-
kled forehead, yellow bushy brows, and pursed lips—provided
him with the impression valued most in a thief: inconspic-
uousness. He had the kind of face no one remembered. One
had but to glance at him to forget his every feature and not
recognize him at the next meeting. This was Seva, a famous
expert on such classic card games as *Terz, Stoss,* and *Bura,*
the inspired interpreter of a thousand card rules to be rigidly
followed. It was said of Seva that he was a "great performer,"
that is, he could demonstrate the dexterity of a card shark. Of
course, he was a card shark, since an honest thief's game is a
game of deceit: watch your partner—that's your right; know
how to cheat; know how to talk your way out of a dubious loss.

They always played in pairs—one on one. None of the experts would lower himself to participate in group games such
as Twenty-one. Seva's partner was Naumov, the brigade
leader of the horse drivers. He was older than his partner (but
then, just how old was Seva? twenty? thirty? forty?). Naumov
had black hair and deep-set black eyes that gave the impression of a martyr. If I hadn't known he was a railroad thief from
the Kuban region I would have taken him for a member of the
religious sect "God Knows" that had been cropping up for decades in the camps. This impression was deepened by the lead
cross that hung from a cord around Naumov's neck—the collar of his shirt was unbuttoned. Nothing blasphemous was intended in the cross. At the time all the thieves wore aluminum
crosses around their necks; it was a kind of symbol, like a tattoo.

In the twenties the thieves wore trade school caps; still

earlier, the military officer's cap was in fashion. In the forties, during the winter, they wore peakless leather caps, folded down the tops of their felt boots, and wore a cross around the neck. The cross was usually smooth but if an artist was around, he was forced to use a needle to paint it with the most diverse subjects: a heart, cards, a crucifixion, a naked woman. . . . Naumov's cross was smooth. It hung on his bare chest, partially blocking the tattoo which was a quote from Esenin, the only poet the "criminal world" recognized:

> *So few my roads,*
> *So many the mistakes.*

"What are you playing for?" Seva spit out his question with boundless contempt; this was considered *bon ton* at the beginning of a game.

"These duds." Naumov tapped his own shoulders.

"Five hundred," Seva appraised Naumov's jacket and pants.

In response there erupted an elaborate stream of obscenities intended to convince the opponent of the much greater worth of the object. The viewers surrounding the players patiently waited for the end of this traditional overture. Seva was not one to fall behind and he swore even more bitterly, trying to lower the price. For his part Seva was "playing" a few secondhand pullovers. After the pullovers had been appraised and cast on the blanket, Seva shuffled the cards.

I was sawing wood for Naumov's barracks together with Garkunov, a former textile engineer. This was night work— after the normal work in the mines. We had to chop and saw enough wood for the day. We came to the horse drivers' barracks immediately after supper; it was warmer here than in our barracks. When we finished, Naumov's orderly gave us some bread and poured cold soup into our pots. It was the leftovers of the single invariable dish of the cafeteria, called "Ukrainian dumplings" on the menu. We would always sit on the floor somewhere in the corner and quickly eat our wages.

We ate in absolute darkness; the barracks' *kolymkas* lit the card-playing area. At the moment we were watching Seva and Naumov.

Naumov lost his "duds." The pants and jacket lay next to Seva on the blanket. The pillow was being played for. Seva's fingernail described elaborate patterns in the air. The cards would disappear in his palm and then appear again. Naumov was wearing an undershirt; his satin Russian blouse departed after the pants. Someone's helpful hands threw a padded jacket over his shoulders, but he cast it off with a jerky movement. Suddenly everyone fell silent. Seva was scratching the pillow with his nail.

"I'll play the blanket," said Naumov hoarsely.

"Two hundred," Seva responded indifferently.

"A thousand, you bitch!" Naumov shouted.

"For what? It's nothing! Junk!" Seva exclaimed. "But for you I'll play it at three hundred."

The game continued. According to the rules it could not be ended until one of the partners had nothing left with which to "answer."

"I'll play the felt boots!"

"Nothing doing," said Seva firmly. "I don't play for regulation-issue rags."

A Ukrainian towel embroidered with roosters and appraised at a few rubbles was played and then a cigarette case with a pressed profile of Gogol. Everything transferred to Seva. The dark skin of Naumov's cheeks reddened.

"On tick," he said obsequiously.

"That's all I need," Seva responded in a lively fashion and stretched his hand back over his shoulder; immediately a lit, homemade cigarette was put into it. Seva inhaled deeply and coughed.

"What am I supposed to do with your 'tick'? No new prisoners are coming in; where can you get anything? From the guards?"

The "rules" didn't oblige Seva to play "on tick," that is, on credit, but Seva didn't want to offend Naumov by depriving him of his last chance to recoup his losses.

"One hundred," he said slowly. "We'll play for an hour."

"Give me a card." Naumov adjusted his cross and sat down. He won back the blanket, pillow, and pants. Then he lost everything again.

"We need some *chifir*," said Seva, putting the things he had won into a large plywood suitcase. "I'll wait."

"Make some, guys," said Naumov. This was an amazing northern drink; several ounces of tea leaves went into one mug—the drink was extremely bitter, drunk in swallows with a snack of salted fish. It totally eliminated any drowiness and therefore was favored by thieves and long-distance truck drivers in the north.

Naumov's heavy black gaze roamed over the surrounding company. His hair was tangled. His gaze fell upon me and stopped. Some thought flashed over his face.

"Come here."

I came out into the light.

"Take off the coat."

It was clear what he had in mind, and everyone watched with interest.

Under the quilted jacket I wore only the regulation undershirt. I'd been issued a field shirt two years earlier, but it had long since rotted away. I got dressed.

"Now you," said Naumov, pointing at Garkunov. Garkunov took off his quilted jacket. His face was white. Beneath the dirty undershirt was a wool sweater. It was the last package from his wife before he was sent off to Siberia, and I knew how Garkunov treasured it. In the bathhouse he would wash the sweater and then dry it on his own body; he never let it out of his hands for a minute, because it would have been stolen immediately.

"Let's have it," said Naumov.

"I won't take it off," said Garkunov hoarsely. "You'll have to take the skin with . . ."

They rushed at him, knocking him down.

"He's biting," someone shouted.

Garkunov slowly got up from the floor, wiping the blood from his face with his sleeve. Immediately Sasha, Naumov's orderly, the same Sasha who had just poured us soup for sawing wood, stooped down and jerked something from the top of his boot. Then he stretched out his hand to Garkunov, and Garkunov sobbed and started to lean over on his side.

"Couldn't we get along without that?" shouted Seva.

In the flickering light of the gasoline lamp, Garkunov's face became gray.

Sasha stretched out the dead man's arms, tore off his undershirt, and pulled the sweater over his head. The sweater was red, and the blood on it was hardly noticeable. Seva folded the sweater into the plywood suitcase—carefully, so as not to get the blood on his fingers. The game was over. I went back to my barracks. Now I had to find a new partner to cut wood with.

A Piece of Meat

>>

YES, GOLUBEV OFFERED this bloody sacrifice. A piece of meat was cut from his body and cast at the feet of the almighty god of the camps. To placate the god. To placate him or to deceive him? Life repeats Shakespearian themes more often than we think. Did Lady Macbeth, Richard III, and King Claudius exist only in the Middle Ages? Shylock wanted to cut a pound of flesh from the body of the merchant of Venice. Is that a fairy tale? Of course, the appendix is but a worm-like spur of the cecum, a rudimentary organ that weighs less than a pound. And, of course, conditions of absolute sterility were observed in offering the bloody sacrifice. . . . The rudimentary organ turned out to be not rudimentary at all, but essential, functional, lifesaving.

The end of the year fills with anxiety the lives of those prisoners who feel insecure about their positions (and who of the convicts feels secure?). The victims of this sense of insecurity were primarily those convicted under Article 58 of the Criminal Code—political prisoners. After years of hungry cold work in the mines they had won the ephemeral uncertain happiness of a few months, a few weeks of work in their chosen profession or any service position—bookkeeper, orderly, doctor, laboratory assistant. They managed to get a position intended for civilians (there were no civilians) or common criminals (common criminals didn't prize these "privileged jobs" since they could always find that type of work, and therefore they frequently got drunk and worse).

Staff positions were filled by persons sentenced under Article 58 of the Criminal Code, and they did their work well. And without hope. For as soon as a commission arrived, they would be removed from their jobs and the head of the camp would be reprimanded. The head of the camp in his turn never wanted to spoil his relations with the senior commission, and removed in advance all those with no right to such privileged jobs.

A good camp head would wait for the commission to arrive, let the commission do its work, remove anyone who had to be removed, and leave. It was not a time-consuming process and anyone not removed would remain, remain for a long time—for a year, till the next December. For a half year at least. A less capable camp head, a more foolish one, would remove such persons in advance so as to be able to report that everything was in order. The worst camp heads, those who had the least experience, would conscientiously carry out the orders of their superiors and not permit persons condemned under Article 58 to work with any instrument other than the pick and wheelbarrow, the saw and the ax. Such camp heads were the least successful. Such camp heads were quickly fired.

Commission raids always occurred toward the end of the year. The higher-ups had their own shortcomings in the control of their operations, and they tried to make up for them toward the end of the year. And they would send commissions. Sometimes they would even come themselves. They would get travel expenses, and the positions under their control would receive individual attention. All they had to do was make a "check" indicating that orders were being carried out. It was just a matter of shuffling from one foot to the other, riding around and on occasion showing their temper, their strength, their magnitude.

From the most insignificant officials to the most important with stars on their shoulders, all maintained this pattern, and both camp inmates and camp heads knew it. It wasn't a new game, and the ritual was a familiar one. Nevertheless it was nerve-racking, dangerous, and irreversible.

This December arrival could "break the backs" and lead to the grave many who were considered lucky only yesterday.

Such raids boded no good for anyone in camp. The convicts, particularly those convicted under Article 58, expected no good. They expected only the worst.

The rumors and fears, those same rumors and fears that always come true, had begun yesterday. Word was out that some higher-ups had arrived with a whole truckload of soldiers and a bus, a "black raven," to haul away prisoners, like booty, to hard-labor camps. Local superiors began to bustle about, and those who had been great became small next to these masters of life and death—these unknown captains, majors, and lieutenant-colonels. The lieutenant-colonel was lurking somewhere in the office depths while the captains and majors scurried about the yard with various lists. Golubev's name was bound to be on those lists. Golubev felt this, knew it. But nothing had been announced yet, no one had been "written off."

About half a year ago the "black raven" had arrived for its

usual raid, its manhunt. Golubev, whose name wasn't on the lists, was standing near the entrance with a convict surgeon. The surgeon worked not only as a surgeon, but also as a general practitioner.

The latest group of trapped, snared, unmasked convicts was being shoved into the bus, and the surgeon was saying good-bye to his friend who was to be taken away.

Golubev stood next to the surgeon and watched the bus crawl away in a cloud of dust to disappear in a mountain ravine. The surgeon looked into Golubev's eyes and said of his friend who had just departed to his death: "It's his own fault. All he needed was an attack of acute appendicitis and he could have stayed."

Those words stuck in Golubev's mind—perhaps not so much the thought, or the logic, as the visual recollection: the firm eyes of the surgeon, the bus cloaked in a cloud of dust . . .

"The duty officer's looking for you." Someone ran up to Golubev to give him the message, and at that moment Golubev caught sight of the duty officer.

"Get your things!"

The duty officer held a list in his hands. It was a short list.

"Right away," said Golubev.

"Meet me at the entrance."

But Golubev didn't go to the entrance. Clutching the right side of his belly with both hands, he groaned and hobbled off in the direction of the first-aid clinic.

The surgeon, that same surgeon, came onto the porch and for a moment something was reflected in his eyes, some distant memory. Perhaps it was the cloud of dust that enveloped the bus that took the other surgeon away forever.

The examination was brief.

"Take him to the hospital. And get me the surgical nurse. Call the doctor from the civilian village as my assistant: It's an emergency operation."

At the hospital, two kilometers from the camp "zone," Golubev was undressed, washed, and registered.

Two orderlies led Golubev into the room and seated him

in the operating chair. He was tied to the chair with strips of
cotton.

"You'll get a shot now," he heard the voice of the surgeon.
"But you seem to be a brave sort."

Golubev remained silent.

"Answer me! Nurse, talk to the patient."

"Does it hurt?"

"It hurts."

"That's the way it always is with a local anesthetic." Golubev heard the voice of the surgeon explaining something to his
assistant. "It's just a lot of talk about it killing the pain. Look at
that. . . ."

"Hold on for a while!"

Golubev's entire body shuddered at the intense pain, but
almost at once the pain was dulled. The surgeons started joking and kidding with each other in loud voices.

The operation was drawing to a close.

"Well, we've removed your appendix. Nurse, show the patient his meat. See?"

The nurse held up to Golubev's face a piece of intestine
about half the size of a pencil.

"The instructions demand that the patient be shown that
the cut was necessary and that the growth was actually removed," explained the surgeon to his civilian assistant.
"This'll be a little bit of experience for you."

"I'm very grateful to you," said the civilian physician, "for
the lesson."

"A lesson in humanity, a lesson in love for one's fellow
man," the surgeon said mysteriously, taking off his gloves.

"If you have anything else like this, be sure to send for
me," the civilian physician said.

"If it's something like this, I'll be sure to," said the
surgeon.

The orderlies, themselves patients in patched white
gowns, carried Golubev into the ward. It was a small
postoperative ward, but there were few operations in the hos-

pital and just then it was occupied by nonsurgical patients.

Golubev lay on his back, carefully touching the bandage that was wrapped around him somewhat in the manner of an Indian fakir or yogi. As a child, Golubev had seen pictures of fakirs and yogis in magazines, and nearly an entire lifetime later he still didn't know if such people really existed. But the thought of fakirs and yogis slid across his brain and disappeared. The exertion of the will and the nervous upheaval were fading away, and the pleasant sense of a duty accomplished filled Golubev's entire body. Each cell of his body sang and purred something pleasant. For the time being he was free from the threat of being sent off to an unknown convict fate. This was merely a delay. How long would the wound take to heal? Seven or eight days. That meant that in two weeks the danger would again arise. Two weeks was a long time, a thousand years. It was long enough to prepare oneself for new trials. Even so, seven or eight days was the textbook period for what doctors refer to as "first intention." And if the wound were to become infected? If the tape covering the wound were to come loose prematurely from the skin? Gingerly Golubev touched the bandage and the hard gauze that was soaked with gum arabic and already drying. He tried to feel through the bandage. Yes . . . This was an extra way out, a reprieve of several days, perhaps months. If he had to.

Golubev remembered the large ward in the mine hospital where he had been a patient a year earlier. Almost all the patients there ripped off their bandages, scratched or pulled open their wounds, and sprinkled dirt into them—real dirt from the floor. Still a newcomer, Golubev was amazed, even contemptuous, at those nocturnal rebindings. A year passed, however, and the patients' mood became quite comprehensible to Golubev and even made him envious. Now he could make use of the experience acquired then.

Golubev drowsed off and awoke when someone's hand pulled the blanket from his face. (Golubev always slept camp fashion, covering his head, attempting above all to keep it warm and to protect it.) A very pretty head with a small mustache and hair cut square in back was suspended above his own. In a word, the head was not at all the head of a convict, and when Golubev opened his eyes, his first thought was that this was some sort of recollection of yogis or a dream—perhaps a nightmare, perhaps not.

"Not an honest crook, not a human being in the whole place," the man wheezed in a disappointed fashion and covered Golubev's face again with the blanket.

But Golubev pulled down the blanket with feeble fingers and looked at the man. The man knew Golubev, and Golubev knew him. There was no mistaking it. But he mustn't rush, rush to recognize him. He had to remember. Remember everything. And Golubev remembered. The man with the hair cut square in back was . . . Now the man would take off his shirt, and Golubev would see a cluster of intertwining snakes on his chest. . . . The man turned around, and the cluster of intertwining snakes appeared before Golubev's eyes. It was Kononenko, a criminal who had been in the same transit prison with Golubev several months earlier. A murderer with multiple sentences, he played a prominent role among the camp criminals and had been "braking" for several years in pretrial prisons. As soon as he was about to be sent off to a forced-labor camp, he would kill someone in the transit prison. He didn't care whom he killed as long as it was not a fellow criminal. He strangled his victims with a towel. A towel, a regulation-issue towel was his favorite murder instrument, his "authorial style." They would arrest him, start up a new case, try him again, and add a new twenty-five-year term to the hundreds of years he already had to serve. After the trial Kononenko would try to be hospitalized to "rest up," and then he would kill again. And everything would begin from the beginning. At that time, execution of common criminals had been abolished. Only "enemies of the people" convicted under Article 58 could be shot.

"Kononenko's in the hospital now," Golubev thought

calmly, and every cell in his body sang joyously, fearing nothing and confident of success. Kononenko's in the hospital now. He's passing through his hospital "cycle"—one of the sinister phases of his metamorphoses. Tomorrow, or perhaps the day after tomorrow, Kononenko's program would demand the usual victim. Perhaps all Golubev's efforts had been in vain—the operation, the fearful straining of the will? Now he, Golubev, would be strangled by Kononenko as his latest victim. Perhaps it was a mistake to evade being sent to a hard-labor camp where they gave you a striped uniform and affixed a six-digit number to your back like an ace of diamonds? But at least you don't get beaten there, and there aren't a lot of Kononenkos running around.

Golubev's bed was under the window. Opposite him lay Kononenko. Next to the door, his feet almost touching Kononenko's, lay a third man, and Golubev could see his face well without having to turn his body. Golubev knew this patient too. It was Podosenov, an eternal resident of the hospital.

The door opened, and the orderly came in with medicine.

"Kazakov!" he shouted.

"Here," shouted Kononeko, getting up.

"There's a note for you." The orderly handed him a folded piece of paper.

"Kazakov?" The name pulsed through Golubev's mind. "He's Kononenko, not Kazakov." Suddenly Golubev comprehended the situation, and a cold sweat formed on his body.

It was much worse than he had thought. None of the three was in error. It was Kononenko under another's name, Kazakov's name and with Kazakov's crimes, and he had been sent to the hospital as a "stand-in." This was even worse, even more dangerous. If Kononenko was Kononenko, Golubev might or might not be his victim. In such a case there was an element of chance, of choice, the opportunity to be saved. But if Kononenko was Kazakov, then there was no chance for Golubev. If Kononenko nursed only the slightest suspicion that Golubev had recognized him, Golubev would die.

"Have you met me before? Why do you keep staring at me like a python at a rabbit? Or maybe like a rabbit at a python? How do you educated people say it?"

Konenenko sat on the stool before Golubev's bed, shredding the note with his fingers and scattering the fragments on Golubev's blanket.

"No, I never laid eyes on you before." Golubev's face was colorless, and his voice hoarse.

"It's a good thing too," said Kononenko, taking a towel from the nail driven in the wall above the bed and shaking the towel before Golubev's face. "I was going to strangle this 'doctor' yesterday." He nodded in the direction of Podosenov whose face was a picture of infinite horror. "Look what the bastard is doing," Kononenko said cheerfully, pointing with the towel in the direction of Podosenov. "See the jar under his cot? He's mixing his own blood with his piss. . . . He scratches his finger and drips in a little blood. Knows what he's doing. No worse than any doctor. And the lab analysis shows he has blood in his urine. Our 'doctor' stays in the hospital. Tell me, is a man like that worthy to live in this world?"

"I don't know."

"You don't know? Yes you do. But yesterday they brought you in. We were together in the transit prison, right? Before my last trial. Then I went under the name of Kononenko."

"I never saw you before," said Golubev.

"Yes you did. That's when I decided. Better I do you in than the 'doctor.' It's not his fault." Kononenko pointed at Podosenov, whose circulation was slowly, very slowly, returning to normal. "It's not his fault. He's only saving his own skin. Just like you or me . . ."

Kononenko walked up and down the room, pouring the paper shreds from one palm to the other.

"And I would have 'fixed' you, sent you to the moon. And I wouldn't have hesitated. But now the orderly brought this note. . . . I have to get out of here quick. Our guys are getting cut up at the mine. They're asking all the thieves in the hospital to help out. You don't understand that kind of life. . . . You don't have the brains to be a crook!"

Golubev remained silent. He knew that life. But only from the outside looking in.

After dinner Kononenko checked out and departed from Golubev's life forever.

While the third bed was empty, Podosenov came over to Golubev's bed, sat down on the edge at his feet, and whispered:

"Kazakov is sure to strangle the both of us. We have to tell the head of the hospital."

"Go to hell," Golubev said.

The Snake Charmer

>>

WE WERE SITTING ON an enormous pine that had fallen during a storm. Trees are barely able to hold themselves upright in the inhospitable earth of the permafrost, and storms easily rip them loose, tearing up their roots, toppling them to the ground. Platonov was telling me of his life here—our second life in this world. I frowned inadvertently when the Jankhar mine was mentioned. I myself had been in rotten, difficult places, but Jankhar's terrible fame was everywhere.

"Just how long were you in Jankhar?"

"A year," Platonov said quietly. His eyes narrowed, and the wrinkles on his forehead became more pronounced. Before me was a different Platonov, older by ten years.

"But I have to admit it was tough only at first, for two or three months. I was the only one there . . . who could read or write. I was the storyteller for the criminal element in camp; I used to retell novels of Dumas, Arthur Conan Doyle, and H. G.

Wells. In exchange they fed and clothed me, and I ate well. You probably made use of that single advantage of an education?"

"No," I said, "I never told 'novels' for soup. I don't even know what that is. I have heard 'novelists' though."

"Is that a condemnation?" asked Platonov.

"Not at all," I replied.

"If I survive," said Platonov, using the same ritualistic formula that introduced any thought concerning things more distant than the next day, "I'll write a story about it. I even have a title: 'The Snake Charmer.' How do you like it?"

"It's good, but first you have to survive. That's the main thing."

Andrei Fyodorovich Platonov, a movie scriptwriter in his first life, died about three weeks after this conversation, died the way many die—swung his pick, stumbled, and fell face down on the stone ground. Proper treatment could probably have returned him to life, because he wheezed on for an hour or more. By the time the stretcher bearers arrived, he was silent and they carried his small body off to the morgue; he was a frail burden of bones and skin.

I loved Platonov because he didn't lose interest in life beyond the blue seas and tall mountains—the life from which we were separated by so many miles and years. We'd almost ceased believing in the existence of that life, or rather, we believed in it the way schoolboys believe in the existence of America. Platonov possessed some books, God only knows how, and he would avoid the usual conversations—what kind of soup there would be for dinner, would we get bread three times a day or all at once in the morning, would the weather be clear tomorrow.

I loved Platonov, and I will now attempt to write his story—"The Snake Charmer."

The end of the working day was by no means the end of work. After the horn sounded, we had to take our tools to the storeroom, turn them in, get in formation, go through two of the ten daily roll calls to the accompaniment of the guards swearing at us and the pitiless abuse and shouts of those of our comrades who were still stronger than us. They too were exhausted and were in a rush to return home and grew angry over every delay. Then there would be still another roll call and we would set out in formation for firewood. It was a five-kilometer walk to the forest, since all the nearby trees had long since been cut and burned. There was a work gang of lumbermen to cut the trees, but the mine laborers had to carry a log each. How heavy logs that even two men couldn't carry were delivered—no one knew. Trucks were never sent for logs, and all the horses were sick in their stalls. A horse weakens and falls ill much quicker than a human being. It often seems, and it's probably true, that man was able to raise himself from the animal kingdom because he had more physical endurance than any of the other animals. It's not correct to say that man has "nine lives" like a cat; instead, one could say of cats that they have nine lives—like a man. A horse can't endure even a month of the local winter life in a cold stall if it's worked hard hours in subzero weather. It's true that the horses of the local Yakut tribesmen don't do any work, but then they don't get fed either. Like the winter reindeer, they dig out last year's dry grass from under the snow. But man lives on. Perhaps he lives by virtue of his hopes? But he doesn't have any hope. He is saved by a drive for self-preservation, a tenacious clinging to life, a physical tenacity to which his entire consciousness is subordinated. He lives on the same things as a bird or dog, but he clings more strongly to life than they do. His is a greater endurance than that of any animal.

Such were Platonov's thoughts as he stood at the gates with a log on his shoulder and waited for a new roll call. They brought and stacked the logs, and people entered the dark log barracks, hurrying, pushing, and swearing.

When his eyes had become accustomed to the dark, Platonov saw that not everyone, by any means, had been at the work site. On the upper berths in the far corner, about seven men were seated in a circle around two others who sat cross-legged in Tartar style playing cards. They'd taken the only light, a kerosene lantern with a smoking wick that quivered as it lengthened the flame and made their shadows sway on the walls.

Platonov sat down on the edge of a bunk. His shoulders and knees ached, and his muscles were trembling. He had been brought to Jankhar just that morning, and it had been his first day at work. There were no vacant spots on the bunks. "When they split up," he thought, "I'll lie down." He dozed off.

When the game on top ended, a black-haired man with a mustache and a long nail on his left little finger leaned over the edge of the bunk. "Okay, send that 'Ivan' over here."

A shove in his back awakened Platonov.

"They're calling you."

"Where's that Ivan?" a voice shouted from the upper bunks.

"My name isn't Ivan," said Platonov, squinting.

"He's not coming, Fedya!"

"What do you mean, he's not coming?"

Platonov was pushed out into the light.

"You plan to go on living?" Fedya asked him quietly as he waved his little finger with the dirty nail before Platonov's eyes.

"I plan to," answered Platonov.

A fist struck him heavily in the face, knocking him to the ground. Platonov stood up, wiping off the blood with his sleeve.

"That's no way to answer," said Fedya mildly. "I can't believe they taught you to answer that way at college, Ivan."

Platonov remaind silent.

"Go over there, scum," said Fedya, "and lie down next to the shit pail. That'll be your place. And if you make any commotion, we'll strangle you." It was no empty threat. Platonov had already seen two men strangled with a towel when the thieves were settling scores. Platonov lay down on the stinking boards.

"How boring, guys!" said Fedya, yawning. "Maybe if I just had someone to scratch my heels. . . ."

"Mashka, hey Mashka, scratch Fedya's heels."

Mashka, a pale pretty boy, dived out into the strip of light. He was a young thief, evidently about eighteen years old.

He pulled off Fedya's worn yellow boots, carefully took off his dirty worn socks, and, smiling, began to scratch Fedya's heels. Fedya giggled and squirmed from the tickling.

"Get out of here," he suddenly said. "You don't know how to tickle."

"But Fedya, I . ."

"Beat it, I said. All he does is scrape you. No tenderness . . ."

The men sitting around him nodded their heads in sympathy.

"I had a Jew in Kosoy—he knew how to scratch! Boy, did he know how to scratch! He was an engineer."

And Fedya grew pensive thinking about the Jewish engineer who scratched heels.

"Fedya, Fedya, how about this new one? Why don't you try him out?"

"His kind doesn't know how to scratch," said Fedya. "Wake him up anyway." Platonov was brought out into the light.

"Fix the lamp, Ivan," ordered Fedya. "Your job will be to put wood on the fire at night and carry out the pail in the morning. The orderly will show you where to dump it. . . ."

Platonov obediently remained silent.

"In exchange," explained Fedya, "you'll get a bowl of soup. I don't eat the swill anyway. Okay, go back to sleep."

Platonov lay down in his former spot. Almost everyone was asleep, huddled together in groups of two or three because it was warmer that way.

"It's so boring my legs are getting longer," mourned

Fedya. "If only someone could tell a novel. When I was in Kosoy . . ."

"Fedya, hey Fedya, how about the new one? Why don't you try him?"

"That's an idea." Fedya came to life. "Wake him up."

Platonov was awakened.

"Listen," said Fedya almost obsequiously, "I shot my mouth off a little."

"That's all right," said Platonov through clenched teeth.

"Listen, can you tell novels?"

Something flashed across Platonov's face. Of course, he could! The cell-full of men awaiting trial had been entranced by his retelling of *Count Dracula*. But those were human beings there. And here? Should he become a jester in the court of the duke of Milan, a clown who was fed for a good joke and beaten for a bad one? But there was another way of looking at the matter: he would acquaint them with real literature, become an enlightener. Even here at the very bottom of the barrel of life he would awaken their interest in the literary word, fulfill his calling, his duty. Platonov could not bring himself to admit that he would simply be fed, receive an extra bowl of soup—not for carrying out the slop pail but for a different, a more noble labor. But was it so noble? After all it was more like scratching a thief's dirty heels than enlightenment.

Fedya waited for an answer, an intent smile on his face.

"I can," Platonov stuttered and smiled for the first time on that difficult day. "I can."

"Oh, sweetie," Fedya livened up. "Come on, crawl up here. Have some bread. You'll eat better tomorrow. Here, sit on this blanket. Have a smoke."

Platonov hadn't smoked for a week, and he received an enormous pleasure from the butt with its home-grown tobacco.

"What's your name?"

"Andrei," said Platonov.

"Listen, Andrei, make it something long and spicy. Something like the *Count of Montecristo*. But nothing about bars."

"Something romantic, maybe?" suggested Platonov.

"You mean Jean Valjean? They told me that one at Kosoy."

"How about *The Club of Black Jacks* then? Or *The Vampire?*"

"There you go. Let's have the Jacks. Shut up, you bastards!" Fedya shouted.

Platonov coughed.

"In the city of Saint Petersburg, in the year eighteen hundred and ninety-three, there occurred a mysterious crime. . . ."

It was almost light when Platonov felt he couldn't go on any more.

"That's the end of the first part," he said.

"That was great!" Fedya said. "Lie down here with us. You won't have much time for sleep; it's already dawn. You can get some sleep at work. Get your strength up for evening . . ."

Platonov fell asleep.

They were being led out to work and a tall country boy who had slept through yesterday's Jacks pushed Platonov viciously through the door.

"Watch out where you're going, you pig!"

Immediately someone whispered something in the boy's ear.

When they were getting into formation, the tall boy came up to Platonov.

"Please don't tell Fedya I hit you. I didn't know you were a novelist, brother."

"I won't tell," said Platonov.

PART FIVE

THE JAILORS' WORLD

Chief of Political Control

>>

THE MACHINE WAILED and wailed and wailed. . . . The alarm
was summoning the hospital director, but the guests were already coming up the stairs. They wore white hospital cloaks,
and the shoulders of the cloaks swelled from the epaulettes
beneath. The hospital garb was too tight for our military
guests.

Two steps in front of them all was a tall, gray-haired man
whose name was known to everyone in the hospital, but whom
no one had ever seen.

It was Sunday for those hospital employees who were not
prisoners, and the hospital director was shooting pool with the
doctors. He was winning; everybody lost to the hospital director.

The director immediately recognized the howling siren,
rubbed the chalk from his sweaty fingers, and sent a messenger to say that he was coming—right away.

But the guests didn't wait.

"We'll start in the Surgical Block. . . ." In the Surgical
Block lay about two hundred persons. Two of the wards held
about eighty patients each. One had straight surgical cases:
closed fractures, sprains, etc. The other had infected cases.
There were also small postsurgery wards and a ward for termi-
nal cases with infections: sepsis, gangrene.

"Where's the surgeon?"

"He went to the village to see his son. The boy goes to
school there."

"Where's the surgeon on duty?"

"He'll be here right away." But the surgeon on duty,
Nurder (whom everyone in the hospital called "Murder"), was
drunk and didn't appear.

The higher-ups were shown around the Surgical Block by the senior orderly, a convict.

"No, we don't need your explanations or case histories. We know how they're written," the official said to the orderly as he walked into the large ward and closed the door behind him. "And don't let the hospital director in for the time being."

One of his aides, a major, took up guard duty at the door to the ward.

"Listen," said the gray-haired official as he stepped out into the center of the ward and gestured at the double row of cots standing along the walls. "Listen to me. I'm the new chief of political control at Far North Construction Headquarters. Anyone who has broken bones as a result of injuries he received either in the mines or in the barracks from foremen or brigade leaders, sing out. We're here to investigate traumatism. The rate of injuries is terrible. But we're going to put an end to it. Anybody who has received such injuries, tell my aide. Major, write it all down!" The major unfolded his notebook and got out a fountain pen.

"Well?"

"How about frostbite, sir?"

"No frostbite, only beatings."

I was the paramedic for the ward. Of the eighty patients, seventy were there with that kind of trauma. It was all written down in their case histories. But not one patient responded to the appeal of the higher-ups. Later on you'd pay for it while you were still lying on your cot. If you shut up, they'd keep you in the hospital for an extra day as payment for your quiet nature and good sense. It was much more advantageous to remain silent.

"A soldier broke my arm."

"A soldier? Can it be that our soldiers beat the prisoners? You can't mean a guard, but some convict work gang leader."

"Yeah, I guess it was a work gang leader."

"See what a bad memory you have? My arrival here is not a run-of-the-mill kind of thing. I'm the boss. And we will not permit beatings! In general, rudeness, hooliganism, and swearing has to come to an end. I already gave a talk at a meeting of the Planning Board. I told them that if the director of Far North Construction is impolite in his conversations with the headquarters chief, and the headquarters chief permits himself to use obscene, abusive language with the director of mines, then how does the mine chief talk to the area heads? It's nothing but a stream of obscenities. But those are still mainland obscenities. The area head chews out his superintendents, work gang leaders, and foremen for using the obscenities of the Kolyma underground world. And what's left then to the foreman or work gang leader? All they can do is take a stick and beat on the workers. Isn't that the way it is?"

"Yes, sir," said the major.

"Nikishov gave a talk at that same conference. He said: 'You're new people. You don't know Kolyma. The conditions here are special. Morality is different here.' But I told him we came here to work and we will work, not the way Nikishov says, but the way Comrade Stalin says."

"That's right, sir," said the major.

When they heard that the matter had reached Stalin, the patients fell silent.

Behind the door was a crowd of area supervisors; they had been summoned from their apartments and were waiting, along with the hospital director, for the speech to end.

"They're removing Nikishov?" Baikov, director of the Second Therapeutic Ward asked quietly, but he was hushed up.

The chief of political control came out of the ward and shook hands with the doctors.

"How about some dinner?" asked the hospital director. "It's on the table."

"No, no," the chief of political control looked at his watch. "I have to make it to the west area, to Susuman by tonight. We have a meeting tomorrow. But maybe . . . I don't want to eat, but here's what we can do. Give me the briefcase." The gray-haired chief took the heavy briefcase from the major's hands.

"Can you give me a glucose injection?"

"Glucose?" asked the hospital director, not under-standing.

"Yes, glucose. An intravenous injection. I haven't drunk anything alcoholic since I was a kid. . . . I don't smoke. But every other day I have a glucose injection. Twenty cubic centi-meters of glucose intravenously. A doctor in Moscow advised me to do it. Keeps me in great shape. Better than ginseng or testosterone. I always carry the glucose with me, but I don't carry a needle; I can get a needle in any hospital. You can give me the shot."

"I don't know how," said the hospital director. "Let me hold the tourniquet. Here's the surgeon on duty; that's right up his alley."

"No," said the surgeon on duty. "I don't know how to do that either. That can't be done by just any doctor, sir."

"Well, how about an orderly?"

"We don't have any nonconvict orderlies."

"How about this one?"

"He's a convict."

"Funny. But what's the difference? Can you do it?"

"I can," I said.

"Sterilize a syringe. . . ."

I boiled a syringe and cooled it. The gray-haired chief took a box with "glucose" from his briefcase, and the hospital direc-tor poured some alcohol on his arm. With the assistance of the party organizer, he broke the glass seal and drew the solution into the syringe. The hospital director attached a needle to the syringe, handed it to me, and tightened the rubber tourniquet on the man's arm; I gave him the shot and pressed the place with a cotton wad.

"I have veins like a truck driver," the chief joked gra-ciously with me.

I said nothing.

"Well, I've rested; it's time to get on the road." The gray-haired chief got up.

"How about the therapeutic wards?" asked the hospital director, afraid that if the guests had to return to examine the therapeutic patients, he would get chewed out for not having reminded them in time.

"There's no reason for us to visit the therapeutic wards," said the chief of political control. "We're pursuing a specific goal on this trip."

"How about dinner?"

"No dinners. Business comes first."

The car of the chief of political control roared to life and disappeared into the frozen dark.

A Child's Drawings

≫≫

THEY DIDN'T HAVE any lists when they took us out for work assignments—just stood us in groups of five, since not all the guards knew their multiplication table. Any arithmetical computation is tricky when it has to be done with live objects in the cold. The cup of convict patience can suddenly overflow, and the administration knew it.

Today we had easy work, the kind they normally reserve for criminals—cutting firewood on a circular saw. The saw spun, knocking lightly as we dumped an enormous log onto the stand and slowly shoved it toward the blade. The saw shrieked and growled furiously. Like us, it detested working in the north, but we kept pushing the log forward until it split into two, unexpectedly light pieces.

Our third companion was chopping wood, using a heavy blue splitting ax with a long yellow handle. He worked on the thicker pieces from the ends, chopped the smaller ones in half with one blow. He was just as hungry as we were and the ax struck the wood in a feeble fashion, but the frozen larch split easily. Nature in the north is not impersonal or indifferent; it is in conspiracy with those who sent us here.

We finished the work, stacked the wood, and waited for the guards. Our guard was keeping warm in the building for which we'd been chopping wood, but we were supposed to march back in formation, breaking up in town into smaller groups.

We didn't go to warm up, though, since we had long since noticed, next to a fence, a large heap of garbage—something we could not afford to ignore. Both my companions were soon removing one frozen layer after another with the adroitness that comes from practice. Their booty consisted of lumps of frozen bread, an icy piece of hamburger, and a torn pair of men's socks. The socks were the most valuable item, of course, and I regretted that I hadn't found them first. "Civvies"—socks, scarfs, gloves, shirts, pants—were prized by people who for decades had nothing to wear but convict garb. The socks could be darned and exchanged for tobacco or bread.

I couldn't reconcile myself with my companions' success, and I too began to use my hands and legs to break off brightly colored pieces of the garbage pile. Beneath a twisted rag that looked like human intestines, I saw—for the first time in my years—a blue school notebook.

It was an ordinary child's drawing book.

Its pages were all carefully and diligently colored, and I began turning the bright cold naive pages, grown brittle in the frost. I also used to draw once upon a time, sitting next to the kerosene lamp on the dinner table. A dead hero of fairy tale would come alive at the touch of the magic brush, as if it contained the water of life.

Looking like women's buttons, the water colors lay in their white tin box, and Prince Ivan galloped through the pine forest on a gray wolf. The pines were smaller than the wolf and Prince Ivan rode him like an Eskimo on a reindeer, his heels almost touching the moss. Smoke spiraled into the blue sky, and the neat Vs of birds could be seen among the stars.

The more I strained to recall my childhood, the more clearly I realized that it would not repeat itself and I would not encounter even a shade of it in the drawing book of another child.

It was a frightening notebook.

The northern city was wooden, its fences and walls painted in a bright ochre, and the brush of the young artist faithfully duplicated the yellow color wherever he wanted to show buildings and creations of man.

In the notebook there were many, very many fences. The people and the houses in almost every drawing were surrounded by even, yellow fences or circumscribed with the black lines of barbed wire. Iron threads of the official type topped all the fences in the child's notebook.

Near the fences stood people. The people in the notebook were not peasants or hunters; they were soldiers, guards, and sentries with rifles. Like mushrooms after the rain, the sentry booths stood at the feet of enormous guard towers. On the towers soldiers walked, their rifle barrels gleaming.

It was a small notebook, but the boy had managed to paint into it all the seasons of his native town.

The ground was bright and uniformly green, as in paintings by the young Matisse, and the blue, blue sky was fresh, pure, and clear. Sunrises and sunsets were conscientiously crimson, and this was no childish inability to capture halftones, color shifts, or shading. Nor was it a Gauguin-type prescription for art where everything that gave an impression of green was painted in the best green color.

The color combinations in the schoolbook were a realistic depiction of the sky in the far north where colors are unusually pure and clear and do not possess halftones.

I remember the old northern legend of how God created the taiga while he was still a child. There were few colors, but they were childishly fresh and vivid, and their subjects were simple.

Later, when God grew up and became an adult, he learned to cut out complicated patterns from his pages and created many bright birds. God grew bored with his former child's world and he threw snow on his forest creation and went south forever. Thus went the legend.

The child remained faithful in his winter drawings as well. The trees were black and naked. They were the enormous deciduous trees of the Daurian Mountains, and not the firs and pines of my childhood.

The northern hunt was on, and a toothy German shepherd strained at a leash held by Prince Ivan. . . . Prince Ivan wore a military hat that covered his ears, a white sheepskin coat, felt boots, and deep mittens. Prince Ivan had a submachine gun slung over his shoulder. Naked, triangular trees were poked into the snow.

The child saw nothing, remembered nothing but the yellow houses, barbed wire, guard towers, German shepherds, guards with submachine guns, and a blue, blue sky.

My companion glanced at the notebook and rubbed a sheet between his fingers.

"Fine some newspaper if you want to smoke." He tore the notebook from my hands, crumpled it, and threw it onto the garbage pile. Frost began to form on the notebook. . . .

The Injector

>>

To: Comrade A. S. Korolyov,
Director of Mines

REPORT

In response to your order requesting an explanation of the six-hour period on the twelfth of November of the current year during which the convict work gang No. 4 under my supervision in the Golden Spring Mine stood idle, I report the following:

The air temperature in the morning was sixty degrees below zero. Our thermometer was broken by the on-duty overseer, as I reported to you earlier. Nevertheless, it was possible to determine the temperature, since spit froze in midair.

The work gang was brought to the site on time, but could not commence work, since the boiler injector serving our area and intended to thaw the frozen ground wouldn't work.

I have already repeatedly brought the injector to the attention of the chief engineer. Nevertheless, no measures were taken, and the injector has now completely gone to pot. The chief engineer refuses to replace the injector just now. We have no place to warm up, and they won't let us make a fire. Furthermore, the guards won't permit the work gang to be sent back to the barracks.

I've written everywhere I could, but I can't work with this injector any longer. The injector hardly works at all, and the plan for our area can't be fulfilled. We can't get anything done, but the chief engineer doesn't pay any attention and just demands his cubic meters of soil.

Mine Engineer L. V. Kudinov,
Area Chief of the Golden Spring Mine

The following was written in neat longhand obliquely across the report:

1. For refusing to work for five days and thus interfering with the production schedule, Convict Injector is to be placed under arrest for three days without permission to return to work and is to be transferred to a work gang with a penal regimen.

2. I officially reprimand Chief Engineer Gorev for a lack of discipline in the production area. I suggest that Convict Injector be replaced with a civilian employee.

Alexander Korolyov,
Director of Mines

Magic

>>

A STICK tapped on the window, and Golubev recognized it. It was the riding crop of the section chief.

"I'm coming," Golubev shouted through the window as he pulled on his pants and buttoned the collar of his shirt. At that very moment the chief's messenger, Mishka, appeared on the threshold of the room and in a loud voice pronounced the usual formula with which Golubev's work day began:

"The chief wants you!"

"In his office?"

"In the guardhouse."

But Golubev was already walking out the door. It was easy working with this boss. He wasn't cruel to the prisoners and, although he inevitably translated any delicate matters into his own crude language, he was intelligent and knew what was what.

True, at that time it was fashionable to show that you had been "reforged" by the new world, and the chief simply wanted to stick to a safe channel in an unfamiliar stream. Perhaps. Perhaps. Golubev didn't give it any thought at the time.

Golubev knew that his boss—his name was Stukov—had been in a lot of hot water with the higher-ups in camp, that a number of accusations had been leveled at him, but he didn't know either the essence or the details of those investigations that had been abandoned.

Stukov liked Golubev for not accepting bribes and for his aversion to drunks—for some reason Stukov hated drunks. . . . Probably he also liked Golubev for his boldness.

A middle-aged man, Stukov lived alone. He loved all sorts

of news about technology and science, and stories of Brooklyn Bridge made him ecstatic. But Golubev couldn't talk about anything even resembling Brooklyn Bridge.

Stukov, however, could learn about that sort of thing from Miller, Pavel Miller—an engineer, convicted of counter revolutionary activity. Miller was Stukov's favorite.

Golubev caught up with Stukov at the guardhouse.

"All you ever do is sleep."

"No, I don't."

"Did you know they brought in a new group of prisoners from Moscow? They came through Perm. I tell you, you were asleep. Get your crew and let's go pick out the ones we need."

The section stood on the very edge of the nonconvict world, at the end of a railroad spur. From there human shipments were sent on through the taiga on foot, and Stukov had the right to select the men who were to be left behind.

Stukov had magical insight, tricks from the area of applied psychology, tricks that he had learned as a supervisor who had grown old working in the labor camps. Stukov needed an audience, and Golubev was probably the only one who could appreciate his extraordinary talent. For a long time this ability seemed supernatural to Golubev—until the moment when he realized he also possessed the magic power.

The camp office permitted them to retain fifty carpenters in the section. The men were lined up in front of the chief, not in a single row, but three and four deep.

Stukov walked slowly down the line, slapping his riding stick against his unpolished boots. From time to time his hand would rise.

"Come forward . . . you. And you. No, not you. You, over there . . ."

"How many have we got?"

"Forty-two."

"Okay, here's eight more."

"You . . . you . . . you."

While the names of the men were copied down, their

"personal files" were also separated out. All fifty were well acquainted with ax and saw.

"Thirty mechanics!"

Stukov walked down the line, slightly frowning.

"Come forward . . . you . . . you. . . . You, get back. What were you arrested for, theft?"

"Yes, citizen chief, for theft."

Thirty mechanics were selected without a single mistake. Ten clerks were needed.

"Can you pick them out by appearance?"

"No."

"Let's go, then."

"You, come forward . . . you . . . you. . . ."

Six men came forward.

"That's all the bookkeepers there are in this group."

They checked the files, and they were right; that's all there were. They selected clerks from other groups that arrived later.

This was Stukov's favorite game, and it amazed Golubev. Stukov was himself as delighted as a child by his magical power and was unhappy whenever he lost his sense of confidence. He didn't make mistakes, but simply lost confidence and then he would stop the selection process.

Each time Golubev watched with pleasure this game that had nothing to do with cruelty or malicious joy at another's misfortune.

Golubev was amazed at this knowledge of people and the unbreakable tie between body and soul.

He had witnessed these demonstrations of his boss's magic power many times. There was no special trick to it— just years of experience in working with convicts. Convict clothes smooth out differences, but that simply lightens the task: to read the profession of a man in his face and hands.

"Who are we going to pick out today, sir?"

"Twenty carpenters. I also got a telegram from headquarters to pick out those who used to work in the secret police," Stukov smirked, "and who were convicted for nonpolitical crimes. That means they'll go back to their desks. What do you think of that?"

"I don't think anything. Orders are orders."

"Did you figure out how I picked out the carpenters?"

"Well . . ."

"I just picked out the peasants. Every peasant is a carpenter. I get good laborers from among the peasants. And I don't make mistakes. But how can I pick out a member of the secret police? I don't know. Maybe they have shifty eyes? What do you think?"

"I don't know."

"Neither do I. Maybe I'll learn by the time I'm old and ready to collect my pension."

The group was mustered, as always, along the row of railroad cars. Stukov made his usual speech about work and the system of work credits, stretched out his hand, and walked twice along the railroad cars.

"I need carpenters. Twenty of them. But I'll pick them myself. Don't move."

"You, come forward . . . you . . . you. . . . That's all of them. Get out their files."

The chief's hand felt for a slip of paper in his jacket pocket.

"Stay where you are. There's one other matter."

Stukov held up the slip of paper.

"Have any of you worked in the secret police?"

Two thousand convicts remained silent.

"I ask you, did any of you work in the secret police?"

From the rear rows, pushing his neighbors aside with his fingers, a thin man made his way to the front. He really did have shifty eyes.

"I worked as an informer, citizen chief."

"Get the hell away from me!" Stukov said with contempt and delight.

My First Tooth

>>

THE COLUMN OF MEN were just as I had dreamed all through my boyhood years. Everywhere were blackened faces and blue mouths burned by the Ural sun in April. Enormous guards leaped into sleighs which flew by without stopping. One of the guards had a single eye and a scar slash across his face. The head guard had bright-blue eyes and we all, all two hundred convicts, knew his name before half the first day had passed—Sherbakov. We learned it by magic, in some unfathomable, incomprehensible way. The convicts uttered his name in an offhand fashion as if it were something they had long been familiar with and this trip with him would last forever. Indeed, he entered our lives for eternity. That is just the way it was—at least for many of us. Sherbakov's enormous, supple figure appeared briefly everywhere. He would run ahead of the column and meet it, and then follow the last cart with his eyes before rushing forward to catch up and overtake it. Yes, we had carts, the classic carts of Siberia. Our group was making a five-day march in convict file. We carried no special goods with us and whenever we stopped anywhere or had to be counted, our irregular ranks reminded one of recruits at a railway station. It would be a long time, however, before the paths of our lives led us to any railway stations. It was a crisp April morning, and our yawning, coughing group was mustered in the twilight of a monastery courtyard before setting out on the long journey.

The quiet, considerate Moscow guards had been replaced by a band of shouting, suntanned young men under the command of the blue-eyed Sherbakov, and we spent the night in the basement of the Solikamsk Police Station which was located in a former monastery. Yesterday, when they poured us into the cold basement, all we could see was ice and snow around the church. There was always a slight thaw in the day and in the evening it would freeze over again. Blue-gray drifts blanketed the entire yard, and to find the essence of the snow, its whiteness, one had to break the hard, brittle crust of ice, dig a hole, and only then scoop out the flaky snow that melted joyously on the tongue and cooled dry mouths, burning them with its freshness.

I was one of the first to enter the basement and was thus able to pick a warmer spot. The enormous icy chambers frightened me, and I searched with all the inexperience of youth for something that would at least resemble a stove. But my chance comrade, a stunted thief by the name of Gusev, shoved me right up against the wall next to the only window, which was barred and had a double frame. Semicircular and about a yard high, the window began down at the floor and looked like a loophole. I wanted to find a warmer spot, but the crowd kept flowing through the narrow door and there was no opportunity to return. Very calmly, without saying a word to me, Gusev kicked the glass with the tip of his boot, breaking first one pane and then the second. Cold air rushed through the new opening, burning like boiling water. Caught in this icy draft and already terribly chilled after a long wait and head count in the courtyard, I began to shiver. Immediately, however, I understood the wisdom of Gusev's action. Of the two hundred convicts, we two were the only ones that night who breathed fresh air. People were so packed into the cellar that it was impossible to lie down or even to sit. We had to remain standing.

The upper half of the room was hidden by a white fog of breath—unclean and stuffy. The ceiling was invisible, and we had no idea if it was high or low. People began to faint. Choking for breath, men tried to push their way to the door, where there was a crack and a peephole. They tried to breathe through it but every now and again the sentry outside the door would shove his bayonet through this peephole, and the men didn't try again after that. Naturally, no medical assistance was rendered to those who fainted. Only the wise Gusev and I were able to breathe easily at the broken window. Muster took a long time. . . .

We were the last to leave and, when the fog in the cellar had cleared, we saw within arm's reach a vaulted ceiling, the firmament of our church-prison. In the basement of the Solikamsk Police Station I found huge letters drawn with a lump of coal, stretching right across the vaulted ceiling: "Comrades! We were in this grave three days and thought we would die, but we survived. Comrades, be strong!"

Accompanied by the shouts of the guards, our column crawled past the outskirts of Solikamsk and made its way toward a low area. The sky was blue, very blue—like the eyes of the guard commander. As the wind cooled our faces the sun burned them so that by nightfall of the first day they became brown. Accommodations, prepared in advance, were always the same. Two peasant huts were rented to put up the convicts for the night. One would be fairly clean, and the other rather dingy—something like a barn. Sometimes it was a barn. The trick was to end up in the "cleaner" one, but that was not for the convicts to choose. Every evening at twilight the commander of the guards would have the men file past him. With a wave of his hand he would indicate where the man standing before him should spend the night. At the time Sherbakov seemed to me to be infinitely wise because he didn't dig around in papers or lists to select "more distinguished criminals," but simply picked out the necessary convicts with a wave of his hand. Later I decided that Sherbakov must be unusually observant; each selection, made by some unfathomable method, turned out to be the correct one. The political prisoners were all in one group, and the common criminals in the other. A year or two later I realized that Sherbakov's wisdom did not depend on miracles. Anyone can learn to assess others by outward appearance. In our group, belongings and suitcases might have served as secondary signs, but our things were being hauled separately, on the carts and peasant sleighs.

On the first night something happened. That event is the subject of this story. Two hundred men stood waiting for the commander of the guards when, off to the left, a disturbance was heard. There was an uproar of shouting, puffing, and swearing, and finally a clear cry of "Dragons! Dragons!" A man was flung out onto the snow in front of the file of convicts. His face was bloodied, and someone had jammed a tall fur hat on his head, but it could not cover the narrow oozing wound. The man, who was probably Ukrainian, was dressed in homespun. I knew him. He was Peter Zayats, the religious sectarian, and he had been brought from Moscow in the same railroad car with me. He prayed constantly.

"He won't stand up for roll call!" the guard reported, excited and puffing.

"Stand him up!" ordered the commander.

Two enormous guards supported Zayats, one on each side. Zayats, however, was heavier, and a head taller than either of them.

"You don't want to stand up? You don't want to?"

Sherbakov struck Zayats in the face with his fist. Zayats spat into the snow.

All at once I felt a burning sensation in my chest and I realized that the meaning of my whole life was about to be decided. If I didn't do something—what exactly, I didn't know—it would mean that my arrival with this group of convicts was in vain, that twenty years of my life had been pointless.

The burning flush of shame over my cowardliness fled from my cheeks. I felt them cool down and my body lighten.

I stepped out of line and said in a trembling voice:

"How dare you beat that man!"

Sherbakov looked me over in sheer amazement.

"Get back in line."

I returned to the line. Sherbakov gave the command, and

heading for the two huts as indicted by his fingers, the group melted away in the darkness. His finger directed me to the poorer hut.

We lay down to sleep on wet, rotting year-old straw which was strewn on bare smooth earth. We lay in each other's embrace because it was warmer that way, and only the criminal element in the group played its eternal card games beneath a lantern hanging from a ceiling beam. Soon even they fell asleep and so, mulling over my act, did I. I had no older friend, no one to set an example. My sleep was interrupted by someone shining a light in my face. One of my comrades, a thief, kept repeating in a confident, ingratiating voice:

"He's the one, he's the one."

The lantern was held by a guard.

"Come on outside."

"I'll get dressed right away."

"Come as you are."

I walked outside shivering nervously and not knowing what was going to happen.

Flanked by two guards, I walked up onto the porch.

"Take your underwear off!"

I undressed.

"Go stand in the snow."

I went out into the snow, looked back at the porch, and saw two rifle barrels aimed directly at me. How much time I spent there that night in the Urals, my first night in the Urals, I don't remember.

I heard a command:

"Get dressed."

As I pulled on my underwear, a blow on the ear knocked me into the snow. A heavy boot struck me directly in the teeth, and my mouth filled with warm blood and began to swell.

"Go back to the barracks!"

I went back to the hut and found my spot, but it was already occupied by another man. Everyone was asleep or pretending to be asleep. The salty taste of blood woudln't go away.

There was some object in my mouth, something superfluous, and I gripped this superfluous thing and tore it forcibly from my mouth. It was a knocked-out tooth. I threw it onto the decaying straw on the earthen floor.

With both arms I embraced the dirty, stinking bodies of my comrades and fell asleep. I fell asleep and didn't even catch cold.

In the morning the group got underway, and Sherbakov's blue imperturbable eyes ranged calmly over the convict columns. Peter Zayats stood in line. No one beat him, and he wasn't shouting about dragons. The common criminals in the group peered at me in a hostile, anxious fashion. In the camps every man learns to answer for himself.

Two days later we reached "headquarters"—a new log house on the riverbank.

The commandant, Nestorov, came out to take over the group. He was a hairy-fisted man, and many of the criminals in the group knew him and praised him highly:

"Whenever they brought in escapees, Nestorov would come out and say: 'So you boys decided to come back! Okay, take your pick—either a licking or solitary confinement.' Solitary had an iron floor, and no one could survive more than three months there, not to mention the investigation and the extra sentence. " 'A licking, sir.'

"He'd wind up and knock the man off his feet! Then he'd knock him down again! He was a real expert. 'Now go back to the barracks.' And that was all. No investigations. A good supervisor."

Nestorov walked up and down the ranks, carefully examining the faces.

"Any complaints against the guards?"

"No, no," a ragged chorus of voices answered.

"How about you?" The hairy finger touched my chest. "How come you're answering as if you had cottonwool in your mouth? And your voice is hoarse."

"No," I answered, trying to force my damaged mouth to

enunciate the words as firmly as possible. "I have no complaints about the guards."

"That's not a bad story," I said to Sazonov. "It's even got a
certain amount of literary sophistication. But you'll never get it
published. Besides, the ending is sort of amorphous."

"I have a different ending," Sazonov said. "A year later
they made me a bigwig in camp. That was when there was all
that talk about rehabilitation and the new society 'reforging'
men. Sherbakov was supposed to get the job of second-in-
command of the section I worked in. A lot depended on me,
and Sherbakov was afraid I still hadn't forgotten about the
tooth I'd lost. Sherbakov hadn't forgotten it either. He had a
large family, and it was a good job, right on top. He was a
simple, direct man and came to see me to find out if I would
object to his candidacy. He brought a bottle of vodka with him
to make peace Russian-style, but I wouldn't drink with him. I
did tell him I wouldn't interfere with his appointment.

"Sherbakov was overjoyed, kept saying he was sorry,
shifting from one foot to the other at my door, catching the rug
with his heel and not able to bring the conversation to an end.

" 'We were on the road, you understand. We had escaped
prisoners with us.' "

"That's not really a good ending either," I said to Sazonov.
"I have a different one then.

"Before I was appointed to the section where I met Sherbakov again, I saw Peter Zayats on the street. He was an orderly in the village. There was no trace of the former young,
black-haired, black-browed giant. Instead he was a limping,
gray-haired old man coughing up blood. He didn't even recognize me, and when I took him by the arm and addressed him
by name, he jerked back and went his own way. I could see
from his eyes that Zayats was thinking his own thoughts,
thoughts that I could not guess at. My appearance was either
unnecessary or offensive to the master of such thoughts who
was conversing with less earthly personages."

"I don't like that variation either," I said.

"Then I'll leave it as I originally had it."

Even if you can't get something published, it's easier to bear a thing if you write it down. Once you've done that, you can forget. . . .

The Lawyers' Plot

>>>

INTO SHMELYOV'S WORK GANG were raked the human rejects; they were the by-products of the gold mine. There were only three paths out of the mine: nameless mass graves, the hospital, or Shmelyov's gang. This brigade worked in the same area as the others, but its assignments were less crucial. Here slogans were not just words. "The Quota Is Law" was understood to mean that if you didn't fill your quota, you had broken the law, deceived the state, and would answer with an additional sentence and even your life. Shmelyov's gang was fed worse, less than the others. But I understood well the local saying, "In camp a large ration kills, not a small one." I wasn't about to pursue the large ration of the leading work gang.

I had only recently been transferred to Shmelyov, about three weeks earlier, and I still didn't know his face. It was the middle of winter and our leader's face was wrapped in a complicated fashion with a ragged scarf. In the evening it was dark in the barracks, and the kerosene lantern barely illuminated the door. I don't even remember our gang leader's face—only his voice that was hoarse as if he had caught cold.

We worked the night shift in December, and each night was a torment. Sixty degrees below zero was no joke. But nevertheless it was better at night, more calm. There were fewer supervisors in the mine, less swearing and fewer beatings.

The work gang was getting into formation to march to work. In the winter we lined up in the barracks, and it is torturous even now to recall those last minutes before going into the icy night for a twelve-hour shift. Here, in this indecisive shoving before the half-opened doors with their cold drafts, each man's character was revealed. One man would suppress his shivering and stride directly out into the darkness while another would suck away at the butt of a homemade cigar. Where the cigar came from was a mystery in a place that lacked any trace of even home-grown tobacco. A third figure would guard his face from the cold wind, while a fourth held his mittens above the stove to accumulate some warmth in them.

The last few men were shoved out of the barracks by the orderly. That was the way the weakest were treated everywhere, in every work gang.

In this work gang I hadn't yet reached the shoving stage. There were people here who were weaker than me, and this provided a certain consolation, an unexpected joy. Here, for the time being, I was still a person. I had left behind the shoves and fists of the orderly in the "gold" gang from which I had been transferred to Shmelyov.

The gang stood inside the barracks door, ready to leave, when Shmelyov approached me.

"You'll stay home," he wheezed.

"Have I been transferred to the morning shift?" I asked suspiciously. Transfers from one shift to another were always made to catch the clock's hour hand so that the working day was not lost and the prisoner could not receive a few extra hours of rest. I was aware of the method.

"No, Romanov called for you."

"Romanov, who's Romanov?"

"This louse doesn't know who Romanov is," the orderly broke in.

"He's in charge. Clear? He lives just this side of the office. You're to report at eight o'clock."

"Eight o'clock?"

An enormous wave of relief swept over me. If Romanov

were to keep me till twelve, when our shift had its dinner, I had the right not to go to work that day. I felt an aching in my muscles and my body was overcome with exhaustion. But it was a joyous exhaustion.

I untied the rope around my waist, unbuttoned my pea jacket, and sat down next to the stove. As its warmth flowed over me the lice under my shirt began to stir. With bit-off fingernails I scratched my neck and chest. And I drowsed off.

"It's time." The orderly was shaking me by the shoulder. "And bring back a smoke. Don't forget."

When I knocked at Romanov's door, there was a clanking of locks and bolts, a lot of locks and bolts, and some unseen person shouted from behind the door:

"Who is it?"

"Prisoner Andreev, as ordered."

Bolts rattled, locks chimed, and all fell silent.

The cold crept under my pea jacket, and my feet lost their warmth. I began to beat one boot against the other. They weren't the usual felt boots but quilted ones, sewn from old pants and quilted jackets.

Again bolts rattled and the double door opened, allowing light, heat, and music to escape.

I stepped in. The door of the entrance hall was not shut and a radio was playing.

Romanov himself stood before me, or rather I stood before him. Short, fat, perfumed, and quick on his feet, he danced around me, examining my figure with his quick black eyes.

The smell of a convict struck his nostrils, and he drew a snow-white handkerchief from his pocket. Waves of music, warmth, and cologne washed over me. Most important was the warmth. The dutch stove was red hot.

"So we meet," Romanov kept repeating ecstatically, moving around me and waving his perfumed handkerchief. "So we meet."

"Go on in." He opened the door to the next room. It contained a desk and two chairs.

"Sit down. You'll never guess why I sent for you. Have a smoke."

He began sifting through some papers on the desk.

"What's your first name?"

I told him.

"Date of birth?"

"1907."

"A lawyer?"

"Actually, I'm not a lawyer, but I studied at Moscow Uni . . ."

"A lawyer, then. Fine. Just sit tight. I'll make a few calls and the two of us will get on the road."

Romanov slipped out of the room, and soon the music in the dining room was shut off. A telephone conversation ensued.

Sitting on the chair I began to drowse and even to dream. Romanov kept disappearing and reappearing.

"Listen, did you leave any things at the barracks?"

"I have everything with me."

"That's great, really great. The truck will be here any minute and we can get on the road. You know where we're going? To Khatynakh itself, to headquarters! Ever been there? It's okay, I'm joking, just joking. . . ."

"I don't care."

"That's good."

I took off my boots, rubbed my toes, and turned my foot rags.

The clock on the wall said 11:30. Even if it was a joke—about Khatynakh—it didn't make any difference: I wouldn't have to go to work today. The truck roared up, the beams of its headlights sliding along the shutters and touching the office ceiling.

"Come on, let's go."

Romanov had donned a white sheepskin coat, a Yakut fur hat, and colorful boots. I buttoned my pea jacket, retied the rope around my waist, and held my mittens above the stove for a moment. We walked out to the truck. It was a one-and-one-half-ton truck with an open bed.

"How much today, Misha?" Romanov asked the driver.

"Seventy degrees below zero, comrade chief. They sent the night shift back to the barracks."

That meant they sent our work gang, Shmelyov's, home as well. I hadn't been so lucky after all.

"All right, Andreev," said Romanov, dancing around me. "Have a seat in back. It's not far. And Misha will drive fast. Right, Misha?"

Misha said nothing. I crawled up onto the truck bed and clasped my knees with my arms. Romanov squeezed into the cab, and we set off.

It was a bad road, and I was tossed around so much that I didn't freeze. In about two hours lights appeared, and we drove up to a two-story log house. It was dark everywhere, and only in one window of the second floor was there a light burning. Two sentries in long leather coats stood next to the large porch.

"Okay, we've arrived. That's great. Have him stand here for the time being." And Romanov disappeared up the large stairway.

It was 2:00 A.M. The lights were extinguished everywhere. Only the desk lamp of the officer-on-duty burned.

I didn't have to wait long. Romanov had already managed to change into the uniform of the NKVD, the secret police. He came running down the stairway and began waving to me.

"This way, this way."

Together with the assistant of the officer-on-duty we went upstairs, and in the corridor of the second floor stopped in front of a door bearing a plaque: "Smertin, Senior Supervisor, Ministry of Internal Affairs." "Smertin" meant "death" in Russian, and so threatening a pseudonym (it couldn't have been his real name) impressed me in spite of my exhaustion.

"For a pseudonym, that's too much," I thought, but we were already entering an enormous room with a portrait of

Stalin that occupied an entire wall. We stopped before a gigantic desk to observe the pale reddish face of a man who had spent his entire life in precisely this sort of room.

Romanov bent politely over the desk. The dull blue eyes of Senior Supervisor Comrade Smertin fixed themselves on me. But only for a moment. He was searching for something on the desk, shuffling some papers. Romanov's willing fingers located whatever it was they were looking for.

"Name?" Smertin asked, poring over the papers. "Crime? Sentence?"

I told him.

"Lawyer?"

"Lawyer."

The pale face looked up from the table.

"Did you write complaints?"

"I did."

Smertin wheezed. "About the bread ration?"

"That and in general."

"Okay, take him out."

I made no attempt to clarify anything, to ask any question. What for? After all I wasn't cold, and I wasn't working the night shift in the gold mine. They could do the clarifying if they wanted to.

The assistant to the officer-on-duty came in with a note, and I was taken on foot through the settlement at night to the very edge of the forest. There, guarded by four towers and three rows of barbed-wire fence, stood the camp prison.

The prison had cells for solitary and group confinement. In one of the latter I related my past history, neither expecting an answer from my neighbors nor asking them about anything. That was the custom—so they wouldn't think I was a "plant."

Morning came. It was the usual Kolyma morning—without light, without sun, and in no way distinguishable from night. A hammer was struck against a rail, and a bucket of steaming boiling water was carried in. The guards came for me, and I said good-bye to my comrades. I knew nothing of them.

They brought me back to the same house, which now appeared smaller than it had at night. This time I was not admitted to Smertin's august presence. The officer-on-duty told me to sit and wait, and I sat and waited until I heard a familiar voice:

"That's fine! That's great! Now you'll get going." On alien territory Romanov used the formal grammatical address in speaking to me.

Thoughts began to stir lazily in my brain. I could almost feel them physically. I had to think of something new, something I wasn't accustomed to, something unknown. This— new thing—had nothing to do with the mine. If we were returning to the Partisan Mine, Romanov would have said: "Now we'll get going." That meant I was being taken to a new place. Let come what may!

Romanov came down the stairs, almost hopping. It seems as if he were about to slide down the bannisters like a small boy. He was holding a barely touched loaf of bread.

"Here, this is for the road. There's something else too." He disappeared upstairs and returned with two herring.

"Everything up to snuff, right? That seems to be about all. Wait, I forgot the most important thing. That's what it means to be a nonsmoker."

Romanov went upstairs and again returned with a small pile of cheap tobacco heaped on a piece of newspaper. About three boxes, I determined with a practiced eye. The standard package of tobacco was enough to fill eight match boxes. That was our unit of measure in camp.

"This is for the road. A sort of dry rations."

I said nothing.

"Have the guards been sent for?"

"They've been sent for," the officer-on-duty answered.

"Have whoever's in charge come upstairs."

And Romanov disappeared up the stairs. Two guards arrived—one an older man with pockmarks on his face and wearing a tall fur hat of the sort worn in the Caucasian Mountains. The other was a rosy-cheeked youth about twenty years old wearing a Red Army helmet.

"This one," said the officer-on-duty, pointing at me.

Both—the young one and the pockmarked one—looked me over carefully from head to toe.

"Where's the chief?" the pockmarked one asked.

"He's upstairs. The package is there too."

The pockmarked man went upstairs and soon returned with Romanov.

They talked quietly, and the pockmarked man gestured in my direction.

"Fine," Romanov said finally. "We'll give you a note."

We walked out onto the street. Next to the porch, on the same spot where the truck from the Partisan Mine had stood the previous night, was a comfortable "raven"—a prison bus with barred windows. I got in, the barred doors closed, the guards occupied their spots in back, and we set off. For a while the "raven" followed the central highway that slices all of Kolyma in half, but then we turned off to the side. The road twisted through the hills, the motor roared on the slopes, and the sheer, pine-forested cliffs with frosty-branched willow shrubs towered above us. Finally, having wound around several hills, the truck followed a riverbed to a small clearing. The trees were cut down, and the edges of the clearing were ringed with guard towers. In the middle, about three hundred yards away, were other slanted towers and the dark mass of the barracks surrounded with barbed wire.

The door of the small guard house on the road opened, and a sentry with a revolver strapped to his waist came out. The bus stopped. Leaving the motor running, the driver jumped out and walked past my window.

"That really twisted us around. It really is a serpent."

I was familiar with the name, and if anything, my reaction was even stronger than to Smertin's name. This was "Serpentine," the infamous pretrial prison where so many people had perished the previous year. Their bodies had not yet decayed. But, then, they never would in the permafrost.

The senior guard went up the path to the prison, and I sat at the window thinking that now my hour, my turn had come. It was just as difficult to think about death as about anything else. I didn't draw myself any picture of my own execution; I just sat and waited.

The winter twilight had already set in. The door of the "raven" opened, and the older guard tossed me some felt boots.

"Put these on."

I took off my quilted boots, but the felt boots were too small.

"You'll never make it in those cloth boots," said the pockmarked man.

"I'll make it."

He tossed the felt boots into the corner of the bus.

"Let's go."

The "raven" turned around and rushed away from "Serpentine." From the vehicles flashing past us I soon realized we were back on the main highway. The bus slowed down, and all around I could see the lights of a large village. The bus stopped at the porch of a brightly lit house, and I entered a lighted corridor very similar to the one in Smertin's building. Behind a wooden barrier next to a wall phone sat a guard with a pistol on his belt. This was the village of Yagodny, named after the head of the secret police. On the first day of our trip we had covered only seventeen kilometers. Where would we go from here?

The guard took me to a far room with a wooden cot, a bucket of water, and a pail that served as a toilet. The door had a hole for observation by the guard.

I lived there two days. I even managed to dry and rewind the bandages on my legs that were festering with scurvy sores.

There was a sort of rural quiet in the regional office of the secret police. I listened intently from my tiny cell, but even in the day it was rare to hear steps in the corridor. Occasionally an outside door would open, and keys could be heard turning in door locks. And there was always the guard—the same guard, unshaven, wearing an old quilted jacket and a pistol in a shoulder holster. It all seemed rather rustic in comparison with gleaming Khatynakh where Comrade Smertin conducted affairs of state. Very, very rarely the telephone would ring.

"Yes, they're gassing up. Yes. I don't know, comrade chief. Okay, I'll tell them."

Whom were they referring to? My guards? Once a day, toward evening, the door to my cell would open and the guard would bring in a pot of soup, a piece of bread, and a spoon. The main course was dumped into the soup and served together. I would take the kettle, eat everything, and lick the pot clean. Camp habits were strong.

On the third day the pockmarked soldier stepped over the cell threshold. He wore a long leather coat over a shorter one.

"Rested up? Let's get on the road."

I stood on the porch of the regional office, thinking we would again have a closed prison bus, but the "raven" was nowhere to be seen. An ordinary three-ton truck stood before the porch.

"Get in."

Obediently I climbed over the side of the bed.

The young soldier squeezed into the cab, and the pockmarked one sat next to me. The truck started up and in a few minutes we were back on the main highway. Where was I being taken? North or south? East or west? There was no sense asking and, besides, the guards weren't supposed to say. Was I being transferred to a different district? Which one? The truck lurched along for many hours and stopped abruptly.

"We'll have dinner here. Get down."

I got down.

We had come to a cafeteria.

The highway was the aorta and main nerve of Kolyma.

Unguarded equipment was constantly being shunted back and forth. Food supplies were always guarded because of the danger of escaped convicts. The guards also provided protection (unreliable, to be sure) from theft by the driver and supply agent.

At the cafeteria one encountered geologists, mine explorers going on vacation with the money they'd earned, and black-market dealers in tobacco and *chifir*—the seminarcotic drink made of strong tea in the far north. These were the heroes and the scoundrels of the north. All the cafeterias sold vodka. People would meet, quarrel, fight, exchange news, and hurry on. Truck motors would be left running while the drivers took a two- or three-hour nap in the cab. One also encountered convicts in the cafeteria. On their way up into the taiga they appeared as clean, neat groups. Coming back, the dirty broken bodies of these half-dead, no longer human creatures were the refuse of the mines. In the cafeteria were detectives whose job it was to capture escapees. The escapees themselves were often in military uniform. Past these cafeterias drove the black limousines of the lords of life and death— the lives and deaths of both convicts and civilians.

A playwright ought to depict the north in precisely such a roadside cafeteria; that would be an ideal setting. I used the idea later in a story, of course.

I stood in the cafeteria trying to elbow my way through to the enormous red-hot barrel of a stove. The guards weren't overly concerned that I would attempt to escape, since it was obvious I was too weak for that. It was clear to everyone that such a goner had nowhere to run to in sixty degrees below zero weather.

"Sit down over there and eat."

The guard brought me a bowl of hot soup and gave me some bread.

"We'll be on our way now," said the young one. "We'll leave as soon as the sergeant comes."

But the pockmarked man didn't come alone. He was with

an older "warrior" (they didn't call them soldiers back then) in a short coat and carrying a rifle. He looked at me, then at the pockmarked man.

"Well, I guess that would be all right," he said.

"Let's go," the pockmarked man said to me.

We went to a different corner of the cafeteria. Bent over by the wall sat a man in a pea jacket and a regulation-issue black flannel cap with ear flaps.

"Sit down here," said the pockmarked man. I obediently sat down on the floor next to this man. He didn't turn his head.

The pockmarked man and the unknown "warrior" left, while the young one, "my" guard, stayed with us.

"They're taking a break, you understand?" the man in the convict hat suddenly whispered to me. "They don't have any right to do that."

"They've long since lost their souls," I said, "so they might as well do whatever they like. What do you care?"

The man raised his head. "I tell you, they don't have the right."

"Where are they taking us?" I asked.

"I don't know where they're taking you. I'm going to Magadan. To be shot."

"To be shot?"

"Yes, I've already been sentenced. I'm from the Western Division—from Susuman."

I didn't like this piece of news at all. But then I didn't know the procedures for applying capital punishment. Embarrassed, I fell silent. The pockmarked soldier walked up with our new traveling companion. They started discussing something with each other. Now that there were more guards, they treated us more roughly. No one bought me any more soup in the cafeterias.

We drove on for a few hours, and three more prisoners were attached to our group. The three new men were of indeterminate age—like all those who had gone through the hell of Kolyma. Their puffy white skin and swollen faces spoke of hunger, scurvy, and frostbite.

"Where are they taking us?"

"To Magadan. To be shot. We've already been sentenced."

We lay bent over in the truck bed, our knees and backs touching. The truck had good springs, the road was well paved so we weren't tossed from side to side, and soon we began to feel the cold.

We shouted, groaned, but the guard was implacable. We had to reach Sporny before morning. The condemned man begged to be allowed to warm himself even for five minutes. The truck roared into Sporny where lights were already burning.

The pockmarked man walked up: "You'll go to the stockade and be sent on later."

I felt cold to the marrow of my bones, was numb from the frost, and frantically beat the soles of my boots against the snow. I couldn't get warm. Our "warriors" kept trying to locate the camp administrator. Finally after about an hour we were taken to the freezing unheated stockade. Frost covered all the walls, and the floor was icy. Someone brought in a bucket of water. The lock rattled shut. How about firewood? A stove?

On that night in Sporny all ten of my toes were again frostbitten. I tried in vain to get even a minute's sleep.

They led us out in the morning and we got back in the truck. The hills flashed by, and approaching vehicles coughed hoarsely in passing. The truck descended from a mountain pass, and we were so warm that we didn't want to go anywhere; we wanted to wait, to walk a little on this marvelous earth. It was a difference of at least twenty degrees. Even the wind was warm, almost as if it were spring.

"Guards! We have to urinate. . . ." How could we explain to the soldiers that we were happy to be warm, to feel the southern wind, to leave behind the ringing silence of the taiga.

"Okay, get down."

The guards were also glad to have an opportunity to stretch their legs and have a smoke. My seeker of justice had already approached the guard:

"Could we have a smoke, citizen warrior?"

"Okay, but go back to your place."

One of the new men didn't want to get down but, seeing that the stop was to be an extended one, he moved over to the edge and gestured to me.

"Help me get down."

I extended a hand to the exhausted man and suddenly felt the extraordinary lightness of his body, a deathly lightness. I stepped back. The man, holding onto the edge of the truck bed, took a few steps.

"How warm!" But his eyes were clouded and expressionless.

"Okay, let's go. It's twenty-two degrees below zero."

Each hour it got warmer.

In the cafeteria of the village of Belyashka, our guards stopped to eat for the last time. The pockmarked man bought me a kilo of bread.

"Here, take it. It's white bread. We'll get there this evening."

A fine snow was falling when far below we saw the lights of Magadan. It was about fifteen degrees above zero. There was no wind, and the snow fell straight down in soft wet particles. The truck stopped in front of the regional office of the secret police, and the guards went inside.

A hatless man wearing civilian clothing came out. In his hands he held a torn envelope. With a clear voice and in the manner of a man accustomed to the job, he called out a name. The man with the fragile body crawled to the side at his gesture.

"To the stockade!"

The man in the suit disappeared into the building and immediately reappeared. In his hands was a new envelope.

"Constantine Ugritsky! To the stockade! Eugene Simonov! Stockade!"

I didn't say good-bye to either the guards or the people who had traveled with me to Magadan. It wasn't the custom.

Only I and my guards now remained at the office porch.

The man in the suit again appeared on the porch with an envelope.

"Andreev! Take him to the division office. I'll give you a receipt," he said to my guards.

I walked into the building. First of all I looked for the stove. There was a steam radiator. Behind a wooden barrier was a telephone and a man on duty. The room was somewhat shabbier than the one at Comrade Smertin's in Khatynakh. But perhaps that room had created such an impression on me because it was the first office I had seen in my Kolyma life? A steep staircase led up to the second floor.

The man in civilian clothes who had handled our group out on the street came into the room.

"Come this way."

We climbed the narrow stairway to the second floor and arrived at a door with the inscription: "Y. Atlas, Director."

"Sit down."

I sat down. In the tiny office the most important area was occupied by a desk. Papers, folders, some lists were heaped on it. Atlas was thirty-eight or forty years old. He was a heavy man of athletic build with receding black hair.

"Name?"

"Andreev."

"Crime, sentence?"

I answered.

"Lawyer?"

"Lawyer."

Atlas jumped up and walked around the desk: "Great! Captain Rebrov will talk to you."

"Who is Captain Rebrov?"

"He's in charge here. Go downstairs."

I returned to my spot next to the radiator. Having mulled over the matter, I decided to eat the kilo of white bread my guards had given me. There was a tub of water with a mug chained to it right there. The windup clock on the wall ticked evenly. Through a half dream I heard someone walk quickly past me and go upstairs, and the officer-on-duty woke me up.

"Take him to Captain Rebrov."

I was taken to the second floor. The door of a small office opened and I heard a sharp voice:

"This way, this way."

It was an ordinary office, somewhat larger than the one in which I had been two hours earlier. The glassy eyes of Captain Rebrov were fixed directly on me. On the corner of the table stood a glass of tea with lemon and a saucer with a chewed rind of cheese. There were phones, folders, portraits.

"Name?"

"Andreev."

"Crime, sentence?"

I told him.

"Lawyer?"

"Lawyer."

Captain Rebrov leaned over the table, bringing his glassy eyes closer to mine, and asked:

"Do you know Parfentiev?"

"Yes, I know him."

Parfentiev had once been my work gang leader back at the mine before I was transferred to Shmelyov's group.

"Yes, I know him. He was my work gang leader, Dmitri Parfentiev."

"Good, so you know Parfentiev?"

"Yes, I know him."

"How about Vinogradov?"

"I don't know any Vinogradov."

"Vinogradov, the director of eastern construction?"

"I don't know him."

Captain Rebrov lit a cigarette, inhaled deeply, and said, extinguishing the cigarette in the saucer:

"So you know Vinogradov and don't know Parfentiev?"

"No, I don't know Vinogradov. . . ."

"Oh, yes, you know Parfentiev and don't know Vinogradov. I see."

Captain Rebrov pushed a button, and the door behind me opened.

"Take him to the stockade."

The saucer with the cigarette and uneaten rind of cheese remained on the right-hand side of the desk next to the pitcher of water in Rebrov's office.

The guard led me through the dark night along the streets of sleeping Magadan.

"Get a move on."

"I have nowhere to hurry to."

"Why don't you chat a little longer?" The guard took out his pistol. "I could shoot you like a dog. It's no problem to write someone off."

"You won't do it," I said. "You'd have to answer to Captain Rebrov."

"Get moving, you louse!"

Magadan is a small town. Together we reached "Vaskov's House," the local prison. Vaskov was second in charge to Berzin when Magadan was being built. The wooden prison was one of the first in Magadan, and the prison kept the name of the man who built it. Magadan had long since acquired a stone prison built according to the latest word in penitentiary technology, but this new building was also called "Vaskov's House." After some brief negotiations at the entrance I was admitted into the yard of "Vaskov's House." I saw a low, stocky, long building made of smooth heavy planks. Across the yard were two wings of a wooden building.

"The second one," a voice behind me said.

I seized a door handle, opened the door, and walked in.

There were double-width berths packed with people. But it wasn't crowded, not shoulder to shoulder. The floor was earthen. A stove made from half a barrel stood on long metal legs. There was a smell of sweat, disinfectant, and dirty bodies. With difficulty I crawled onto an upper berth where it was warmer and found a free spot. My neighbor woke up.

"Straight from the woods?"

"Yes."

"With fleas?"

"With fleas."

"Then lie down in the corner. The disinfection service is working here, and we don't have fleas."

"Disinfection—that's good," I thought. "And mainly, it's warm."

We were fed in the morning. There was bread and boiling water. I wasn't yet due to get bread. I took off my quilted boots, put them under my head, lowered my padded trousers to keep my feet warm, fell asleep, and woke up twenty-four hours later. Bread was being passed out and I was already registered for meals in "Vaskov's House."

For dinner they gave broth and three spoons of wheat kasha. I slept till morning of the next day when the hysterical voice of the guard on duty awakened me.

I crawled down from the bunk.

"Go outside—to that porch over there."

The doors of the true "House of Vaskov" opened before me, and I entered a low, dimly lit corridor. The guard turned the lock, threw back the massive iron latch, and disclosed a tiny cell with a double berth. Two men sat bent over in the corner on the lower bunk.

I walked up to the window and sat down. Someone was shaking me by the shoulders. It was my gang leader, Dmitri Parfentiev, whom Rebrov had asked about.

"Do you understand anything?"

"Nothing."

"When were you brought in?"

"Three days ago. Atlas had me brought in a small truck."

"Atlas? He questioned me in the division office. About forty years old, balding, in civilian clothing."

"With me he wore a military uniform."

"What did Captain Rebrov ask you?"

"Do I know Vinogradov."

"Well?"

"How am I supposed to know him?"

"Vinogradov is the director of eastern construction."

"You know that, but I don't know who Vinogradov is."

"He and I were students at the same school."

I began to put two and two together. Before his arrest Parfentiev had been a district prosecutor. Vinogradov, in passing through the area, learned that his university friend was in the mine and sent him some money. He also asked the head of the mine to help Parfentiev. The mine doctor had told Smertin and Smertin told Rebrov, who started an investigation of Vinogradov. All convicts in the northern mines who had formerly been lawyers were brought in. The rest was simply a matter of the usual investigative techniques.

"But why are we here? I was in wing . . ."

"We're being released," said Parfentiev.

"Released? Being let go, that is, not being let go but being sent to a transit prison?"

"Yes," said a third man, crawling out into the light and looking me over with obvious contempt.

He had a fat repulsive pink face and was dressed in a black fur coat. His voile shirt was open at the chest.

"So you know each other? Captain Rebrov didn't have time to squash you. An enemy of the people . . ."

"What are you, a friend of the people?"

"At least I'm not a political prisoner. I was never in the secret police and I never did anything to the working people. But it's because of your kind that we go to jail."

"What are you, a thief?" I asked.

"Maybe."

"Okay, stop it, stop it," Parfentiev broke in.

The doors clanked open.

"Come on out!"

There were about seven men standing at the entrance. Parfentiev and I walked up to them.

"Are all of you lawyers?" asked Parfentiev.

"Yes! Yes!"

"What happened? Why are we being released?"

Some all-knowing soul said quietly:

"Captain Rebrov has been arrested. Everyone arrested under his instructions is being released."

PART SIX

THE AMERICAN CONNECTION

Lend-Lease

>>

THE FRESH TRACTOR PRINTS in the marsh were tracks of some prehistoric beast that bore little resemblance to an article of American technology delivered under the terms of Lend-Lease.

We convicts had heard of these gifts from beyond the sea and the emotional confusion they had introduced into the minds of the camp bigwigs. Worn knit suits and secondhand pullovers collected for the convicts of Kolyma were snapped up in near fistfights by the wives of the Magadan generals.

As for the magical jars of sausage sent by Lend-Lease, we saw them only at a distance. What we knew and knew well were the chubby tins of Spam. Counted, measured by a very complex table of replacement, stolen by the greedy hands of the camp authorities, counted again and measured a second time before introduction to the kettle, boiled there till transformed into mysterious fibers that smelled like anything in the world except meat—this Spam excited the eye, but not the taste buds. Once tossed in the pot, Spam from Lend-Lease had no taste at all. Convict stomachs preferred something domestic such as old, rotten venison that couldn't be boiled down even in seven camp kettles. Venison doesn't disappear, doesn't become ephemeral like Spam.

Oatmeal from Lend-Lease we relished, but we never got more than two tablespoons per portion.

But the fruits of technology also came from Lend-Lease—fruits that could not be eaten: clumsy tomahawk-like hatchets, handy shovels with un-Russian work-saving handles. The shovel blades were instantaneously affixed to long Russian handles and flattened to make them more capacious.

Barrels of glycerin! Glycerin! The guard dipped out a bucketful with a kitchen pot on the very frist night and got rich selling it to the convicts as "American honey."

From Lend-Lease also came enormous black fifty-ton Diamond trucks with trailers and iron sides and five-ton Studebakers that could easily manage any hill. There were no better trucks in all of Kolyma. Day and night, Studebakers and Diamonds hauled American wheat along the thousand-mile road. The wheat was in pretty white linen sacks stamped with the American eagle, and chubby, tasteless bread "rations" were baked from this flour. Bread from Lend-Lease flour possessed an amazing quality: anyone who ate it stopped visiting the toilet; once in five days a bowel movement would be produced that wasn't even worth the name. The stomach and intestines of the convict absorbed without remainder this magnificent white bread with its mixture of corn, bone meal, and something else in addition—perhaps hope. And the time has not yet come to count the lives saved by this wheat from beyond the sea.

The Studebakers and Diamonds ate a lot of gas, but the gas also came from Lend-Lease, a light aviation gas. Russian trucks were adapted to be heated with wood: two stoves set near the motor were heated with split logs. There arose several wood supply centers headed by party members working on contract. Technical leadership at these wood supply centers was provided by a chief engineer, a plain engineer, a rate setter, a planner, and bookkeepers. I don't remember whether two or three laborers ran the circular saw at the wood-processing plant. There may have been as many as three. The equipment was from Lend-Lease, and when a tractor came to the camp, a new word appeared in our language: "bulldozer."

The prehistoric beast was freed from its chain: an American bulldozer with caterpillar tracks and a wide blade. The vertical metal shield gleamed like a mirror reflecting the sky, the trees, the stars, and the dirty faces of the convicts. Even the guard walked up to the foreign monster and said a man could shave himself before such a mirror. But there was no shaving for us; even the thought couldn't have entered our heads.

The sighs and groans of the new American beast could be heard for a long time in the frosty air. The bulldozer coughed angrily in the frost, puffed, and then suddenly roared and moved boldly forward, crushing the shrubbery and passing easily over the stumps; this then was the help from beyond the sea.

Everywhere on the slope of the mountain were scattered construction-quality logs and firewood. Now we would not have the unbearable task of hauling and stacking the iron logs of Daurian larch by hand. To drag the logs over the shrubbery, down the narrow paths of the mountain slope, was an impossible job. Before 1938 they used to send horses for the job, but horses could not tolerate the north as well as people, were weaker than people, died under the strain of the hauling. Now the vertical knife of the foreign bulldozer had come to help us (us?).

None of us ever imagined that we would be given some light work instead of the unendurable log hauling that was hated by all. They would simply increase our norms and we would be forced to do something else—just as degrading and contemptible as any camp labor. Our frostbitten toes and fingers would not be cured by the American bulldozer. But there was the American machine grease! Ah yes, the machine grease! The barrel was immediately attacked by a crowd of starving men who knocked out the bottom right on the spot with a stone.

In their hunger, they claimed the machine grease was butter sent by Lend-Lease and there remained less than half a barrel by the time a sentry was sent to guard it and the camp administration drove off the crowd of starving, exhausted men with rifle shots. The fortunate ones gulped down this Lend-Lease butter, not believing it was simply machine grease. After all, the healing American bread was also tasteless and also had that same metallic flavor. And everyone who had been lucky enough to touch the grease licked his fingers hours later, gulping down the minutest amounts of the foreign joy that tasted like young stone. After all, a stone is not born a stone, but a soft oily creature. A creature, and not a thing. A stone becomes a thing in old age. Young wet limestone tuffs in the mountains enchanted the eyes of escaped convicts and workers from the geological surveys. A man had to exert his will to tear himself away from these honeyed shores, these milky rivers of flowing young stone. But that was a mountain, a valley, stone; and this was a delivery from Lend-Lease, the creation of human hands. . . .

Nothing terrible happened to those who had dipped their hands into the barrel. Trained in Kolyma, stomach and bowels proved themselves capable of coping with machine grease. A sentry was placed to guard the remainder, for this was food for machines—creatures infinitely more important to the state than people.

And thus from beyond the ocean there had arrived one of those creatures as a symbol of victory, friendship, and something else.

Three hundred men felt boundless envy toward the prisoner sitting at the wheel of the American tractor—Grinka Lebedev. There were better tractor operators than Lebedev among the convicts, but they had all been convicted according to Article 58 of the Criminal Code (political prisoners). Grinka Lebedev was a common criminal, a parricide to be precise. Each of the three hundred witnessed his earthly joy: to roar over to the logging area sitting at the wheel of a well-lubricated tractor.

The logging area kept moving back. Felling the taller trees suitable for building materials in Kolyma takes place along the stream banks where deep ravines force the trees to reach upward from their wind-protected havens toward the sun. In windy spots, in bright light, on marshy mountain slopes stand dwarfs—broken, twisted, tormented from eternally turning after the sun, from their constant struggle for a piece of thawed ground. The trees on the mountain slopes don't look like trees, but like monsters fit for a sideshow. Felling trees is similar to mining gold in those same streams in that it is just as rushed: the stream, the pan, the launder, the temporary barracks, the hurried predatory leap that leaves the stream and area without forest for three hundred years and without gold—forever.

Somewhere there exists the science of forestry, but what kind of forestry can there be in a three-hundred-year-old larch forest in Kolyma during the war when the response to Lend-Lease is a hurried plunge into gold fever, harnessed, to be sure, by the guard towers of the "zones."

Many tall trees and even prepared, sectioned firelogs were abandoned. Many thick-ended logs disappeared into the snow, falling to the ground as soon as they had been hoisted onto the sharp, brittle shoulders of the prisoners. Weak prisoner hands, tens of hands cannot lift onto a shoulder (there exists no such shoulder!) a two-meter log, drag its iron weight for tens of meters over shrubs, potholes, and pits. Many logs had been abandoned because of the impossibility of the job, and the bulldozer was supposed to help us.

But for its first trip in the land of Kolyma, on Russian land, it had been assigned a totally different job.

We watched the chugging bulldozer turn to the left and begin to climb the terrace to where there was a projection of rock and where we had been taken to work hundreds of times along the old road that led past the camp cemetery.

I hadn't given any thought to why we were led to work for the last few weeks along a new road instead of the familiar path indented from the boot heels of the guards and the thick rubber galoshes of the prisoners. The new road was twice as long as the old one. Everywhere there were hills and dropoffs, and we exhausted ourselves just getting to the job. But no one asked why we were being taken by a new path.

That was the way it had to be; that was the order; and we

crawled on all fours, grabbing at stones that ripped open the skin of the fingers till the blood ran.

Only now did I see and understand the reason for all of this, and I thank God that He gave me the time and strength to witness it.

The logging area was just ahead, the slope of the mountain had been laid bare, and the shallow snow had been blown away by the wind. The stumps had all been rooted out; a charge of ammonal was placed under the larger ones, and the stump would fly into the air. Smaller stumps were uprooted with long bars. The smallest were simply pulled out by hand like the shrubs of dwarf cedar. . . .

The mountain had been laid bare and transformed into a gigantic stage for a camp mystery play.

A grave, a mass prisoner grave, a stone pit stuffed full with undecaying corpses of 1938 was sliding down the side of the hill, revealing the secret of Kolyma.

In Kolyma, bodies are not given over to earth, but to stone. Stone keeps secrets and reveals them. The permafrost keeps and reveals secrets. All of our loved ones who died in Kolyma, all those who were shot, beaten to death, sucked dry by starvation, can still be recognized even after tens of years. There were no gas furnaces in Kolyma. The corpses wait in stone, in the permafrost.

In 1938 entire work gangs dug such graves, constantly drilling, exploding, deepening the enormous gray, hard, cold stone pits. Digging graves in 1938 was easy work; there was no "assignment," no "norm" calculated to kill a man with a fourteen-hour working day. It was easier to dig graves than to stand in rubber galoshes over bare feet in the icy waters where they mined gold—the "basic unit of production," the "first of all metals."

These graves, enormous stone pits, were filled to the brim with corpses. The bodies had not decayed; they were just bare skeletons over which stretched dirty, scratched skin bitten all over by lice.

The north resisted with all its strength this work of man, not accepting the corpses into its bowels. Defeated, humbled, retreating, stone promised to forget nothing, to wait and preserve its secret. The severe winters, the hot summers, the winds, the six years of rain had not wrenched the dead men from the stone. The earth opened, baring its subterranean storerooms, for they contained not only gold and lead, tungsten and uranium, but also undecaying human bodies.

These human bodies slid down the slope, perhaps attempting to arise. From a distance, from the other side of the creek, I had previously seen these moving objects that caught up against branches and stones; I had seen them through the few trees still left standing and I thought that they were logs that had not yet been hauled away.

Now the mountain was laid bare, and its secret was revealed. The grave "opened," and the dead men slid down the stony slope. Near the tractor road an enormous new common grave was dug. Who had dug it? No one was taken from the barracks for this work. It was enormous, and I and my companions knew that if we were to freeze and die, place would be found for us in this new grave, this housewarming for dead men.

The bulldozer scraped up the frozen bodies, thousands of bodies of thousands of skeleton-like corpses. Nothing had decayed: the twisted fingers, the pus-filled toes which were reduced to mere stumps after frostbite, the dry skin scratched bloody and eyes burning with a hungry gleam.

With my exhausted, tormented mind I tried to understand: How did there come to be such an enormous grave in this area? I am an old resident of Kolyma, and there hadn't been any gold mine here as far as I knew. But then I realized that I knew only a fragment of that world surrounded by a barbed-wire zone and guard towers that reminded one of the pages of tent-like Moscow architecture. Moscow's taller buildings are guard towers keeping watch over the city's prisoners. That's what those buildings look like. And what served as models for Moscow architecture—the watchful towers of the Moscow Kremlin or the guard towers of the camps? The guard towers of the camp "zone" represent the main concept advanced by their time and brilliantly expressed in the symbolism of architecture.

I realized that I knew only a small bit of that world, a pitifully small part, that twenty kilometers away there might be a shack for geological explorers looking for uranium or a gold mine with thirty thousand prisoners. Much can be hidden in the folds of the mountain.

And then I remembered the greedy blaze of the fireweed, the furious blossoming of the taiga in summer when it tried to hide in the grass and foliage any deed of man—good or bad. And if I forget, the grass will forget. But the permafrost and stone will not forget.

Grinka Lebedev, parricide, was a good tractor driver, and he controlled the well-oiled foreign tractor with ease. Grinka Lebedev carefully carried out his job, scooping the corpses toward the grave with the gleaming bulldozer knife-shield, pushing them into the pit and returning to drag up more.

The camp administration had decided that the first job for the bulldozer received from Lend-Lease should not be work in the forest, but something far more important.

The work was finished. The bulldozer heaped a mound of stones and gravel on the new grave, and the corpses were hidden under stone. But they did not disappear.

The bulldozer approached us. Grinka Lebedev, common criminal and parricide, did not look at us, prisoners of Article 58. Grinka had been entrusted with a task by the government, and he had fulfilled that task. On the stone face of Grinka Lebedev were hewn pride and a sense of having accomplished his duty.

The bulldozer roared past us; on the mirror-like blade there was no scratch, not a single spot.

Condensed Milk

>>>

ENVY, like all our feelings, had been dulled and weakened by hunger. We lacked the strength to experience emotions, to seek easier work, to walk, to ask, to beg. . . . We envied only our acquaintances, the ones who had been lucky enough to get office work, a job in the hospital or the stables—wherever there was none of the long physical labor glorified as heroic and noble in signs above all the camp gates. In a word, we envied only Shestakov.

External circumstances alone were capable of jolting us out of apathy and distracting us from slowly approaching death. It had to be an external and not an internal force. Inside there was only an empty scorched sensation, and we were indifferent to everything, making plans no further than the next day.

Even now I wanted to go back to the barracks and lie down on the bunk, but instead I was standing at the doors of the commissary. Purchases could be made only by petty criminals and thieves who were repeated offenders. The latter were classified as "friends of the people." There was no reason for us politicals to be there, but we couldn't take our eyes off the loaves of bread that were brown as chocolate. Our heads swam from the sweet heavy aroma of fresh bread that tickled the nostrils. I stood there, not knowing when I would find the strength within myself to return back to the barracks. I was staring at the bread when Shestakov called to me.

I'd known Shestakov on the "mainland," in Butyr Prison where we were cellmates. We weren't friends, just acquaintances. Shestakov didn't work in the mine. He was an engineer-geologist, and he was taken into the prospecting group—in the office. The lucky man barely said hello to his Moscow acquaintances. We weren't offended. Everyone looked out for himself here.

"Have a smoke," Shestakov said and he handed me a scrap of newspaper, sprinkled some tobacco on it, and lit a match, a real match.

I lit up.

"I have to talk to you," Shestakov said.

"To me?"

"Yeah."

We walked behind the barracks and sat down on the lip of the old mine. My legs immediately became heavy, but Shestakov kept swinging his new regulation-issue boots that smelled slightly of fish grease. His pant legs were rolled up, revealing checkered socks. I stared at Shestakov's feet with sincere admiration, even delight. At least one person from our cell didn't wear foot rags. Under us the ground shook from dull explosions; they were preparing the ground for the night shift. Small stones fell at our feet, rustling like unobtrusive gray birds.

"Let's go farther," said Shestakov.

"Don't worry, it won't kill us. Your socks will stay in one piece."

"That's not what I'm talking about," said Shestakov and swept his index finger along the line of the horizon. "What do you think of all that?"

"It's sure to kill us," I said. It was the last thing I wanted to think of.

"Nothing doing. I'm not willing to die."

"So?"

"I have a map," Shestakov said sluggishly. "I'll make up a group of workers, take you and we'll go to Black Springs. That's fifteen kilometers from here. I'll have a pass. And we'll make a run for the sea. Agreed?"

He recited all this as indifferently as he did quickly.

"And when we get to the sea? What then? Swim?"

"Who cares. The important thing is to begin. I can't live

like this any longer. 'Better to die on your feet than live on your knees.' " Shestakov pronounced the sentence with an air of pomp. "Who said that?"

It was a familiar sentence. I tried, but lacked the strength to remember who had said those words and when. All that smacked of books was forgotten. No one believed in books.

I rolled up my pants and showed the breaks in the skin from scurvy.

"You'll be all right in the woods," said Shestakov. "Berries, vitamins. I'll lead the way. I know the road. I have a map."

I closed my eyes and thought. There were three roads to the sea from here—all of them five hundred kilometers long, no less. Even Shestakov wouldn't make it, not to mention me. Could he be taking me along as food? No, of course not. But why was he lying? He knew all that as well as I did. And suddenly I was afraid of Shestakov, the only one of us who was working in the field in which he'd been trained. Who had set him up here and at what price? Everything here had to be paid for. Either with another man's blood or another man's life.

"Okay," I said, opening my eyes. "But I need to eat and get my strength up."

"Great, great. You definitely have to do that. I'll bring you some . . . canned food. We can get it. . . ."

There are a lot of canned foods in the world—meat, fish, fruit, vegetables. . . . But best of all was condensed milk. Of course, there was no sense drinking it with hot water. You had to eat it with a spoon, smear it on bread, or swallow it slowly, from the can, eat it little by little, watching how the light liquid mass grew yellow and how a small sugar star would stick to the can. . . .

"Tomorrow," I said, choking from joy. "Condensed milk."

"Fine, fine, condensed milk." And Shestakov left.

I returned to the barracks and closed my eyes. It was hard to think. For the first time I could visualize the material nature of our psyche in all its palpability. It was painful to think, but necessary.

He'd make a group for an escape and turn everyone in.

That was crystal clear. He'd pay for his office job with our blood, with my blood. They'd either kill us there, at Black Springs, or bring us in alive and give us an extra sentence— ten or fifteen years. He couldn't help but know that there was no escape. But the milk, the condensed milk . . .

I fell asleep and in my ragged hungry dreams saw Shesta- kov's can of condensed milk, a monstrous can with a sky-blue label. Enormous and blue as the night sky, the can had a thousand holes punched in it, and the milk seeped out and flowed in a stream as broad as the Milky Way. My hands easily reached the sky and greedily I drank the thick, sweet, starry milk.

I don't remember what I did that day nor how I worked. I waited. I waited for the sun to set in the west and for the horses to neigh, for they guessed the end of the work day bet- ter than people.

The work horn roared hoarsely, and I set out for the bar- racks where I found Shestakov. He pulled two cans of con- densed milk from his pockets.

I punched a hole in each of the cans with the edge of an ax, and a thick white stream flowed over the lid onto my hand.

"You should punch a second hole for the air," said Shesta- kov.

"That's all right," I said, licking my dirty sweet fingers.

"Let's have a spoon," said Shestakov, turning to the la- borers surrounding us. Licked clean, ten glistening spoons were stretched out over the table. Everyone stood and watched as I ate. No one was indelicate about it, nor was there the slightest expectation that they might be permitted to partici- pate. None of them could even hope that I would share this milk with them. Such things were unheard of, and their inter- est was absolutely selfless. I also knew that it was impossible not to stare at food disappearing in another man's mouth. I sat down so as to be comfortable and drank the milk without any bread, washing it down from time to time with cold water. I finished both cans. The audience disappeared—the show was over. Shestakov watched me with sympathy.

"You know," I said, carefully licking the spoon, "I changed my mind. Go without me."

Shestakov comprehended immediately and left without saying a word to me.

It was, of course, a weak, worthless act of vengeance just like all my feelings. But what else could I do? Warn the others? I didn't know them. But they needed a warning. Shestakov managed to convince five people. They made their escape the next week; two were killed at Black Springs and the other three stood trial a month later. Shestakov's case was considered separately "because of production considerations." He was taken away, and I met him again at a different mine six months later. He wasn't given any extra sentence for the escape attempt; the authorities played the game honestly with him even though they could have acted quite differently.

He was working in the prospecting group, was shaved and well fed, and his checkered socks were in one piece. He didn't say hello to me, but there was really no reason for him to act that way. I mean, after all, two cans of condensed milk aren't such a big deal.

PART SEVEN

RELEASE

Esperanto

>>

A WANDERING ACTOR who happened to be a prisoner reminded me of this story. It was just after a performance put on by the camp activities group in which he was the main actor, producer, and theater carpenter.

He mentioned the name Skoroseev, and I immediately recalled the road to Siberia in '39. The five of us had endured the typhoid quarantine, the work assignments, the roll calls in the biting frost, but we were nevertheless caught up by the camp nets and cast out into the endlessness of the taiga.

We five neither knew nor wanted to know anything about each other until our group reached the spot where we were to work and live. Each of us received the news of our future trip in his own way: one went mad, thinking he was to be shot at the very moment he was granted life. Another tried to talk his way out of the situation, and almost succeeded. I was the third—an indifferent skeleton from the gold mine. The fourth was a jack-of-all-trades over seventy years old. The fifth was Skoroseev. "Skoroseev," he would pronounce carefully, standing on tiptoes so as to look each of us in the eye.

I couldn't care less, but the jack-of-all-trades kept up the conversation.

"What kind of work did you do before?"

"I was an agronomist in the People's Agriculture Commissariat."

The chief of coal exploration, whose responsibility it was to receive the group, leafed though Skoroseev's folder.

"I can still work, citizen chief. . . ."

"Okay, I'll make you a watchman. . . ."

Skoroseev performed his duties zealously. Not for a minute would he leave his post, afraid that any mistake could be exploited by a fellow prisoner and reported to the camp authorities. It was better not to take any chances.

Once there was a heavy snowstorm that lasted all night. Skoroseev's replacement was a Gallician by the name of Narynsky. This chestnut-haired convict had been a prisoner of war during World War I, and he had been convicted of plotting to reestablish Austro-Hungary. He was a little proud of having been accused of such a "crime" among the throngs of Trotskyites and saboteurs. Narynsky told us with a chuckle that when he took over the watch he discovered that Skoroseev hadn't budged from his spot even during the snowstorm. Skoroseev's dedication was noticed, and his position became more secure.

Once a horse died in camp. It was no great loss, since horses work poorly in the far north. But the meat! The meat! The hide had to be removed from the frozen carcass. There were neither butchers nor volunteers, but Skoroseev offered to do the job. The camp chief was surprised and pleased; there would be both hide and meat! The hide could be registered in the official report, and the meat would go into the general pot. The entire barracks, all of the village spoke of Skoroseev. Meat! meat! The carcass was dragged into the bathhouse, where Skoroseev skinned and gutted it when it had thawed. The hide stiffened again in the frost and was carried off to the storehouse. We never tasted the meat; at the last minute the camp chief realized that there was no veterinarian who could sign to give permission. An official report was made up, and the carcass was hacked into pieces and burned on a bonfire in the presence of the camp chief and the work gang leader.

We were prospecting for coal, but without any luck. Little by little, in groups of five and ten, people were taken away from our camp. Making their way along the forest path up the mountain, these people left my life forever. Each of us understood that ours was a prospecting group and not a mine group. Each strove to remain here, to "brake," as long as possible. One would work with unusual diligence, another would pray longer than usual. Anxiety had entered our lives.

A new group of guards had arrived from behind the mountain. For us? But they took no one away, no one!

That night there was a search in the barracks. We had no books, no knives, no felt pens, no newspapers, no writing paper. What was there to search for?

They were confiscating civilian clothing. Many of the prisoners had acquired such clothing from civilians who worked in the prospecting group which itself was unguarded. Were they trying to prevent escapes? Fulfilling an order, maybe? Or was there some change of authority higher on up?

Everything was confiscated without any reports or records. Confiscated, and that was that! Indignation was boundless. I recalled how, two years earlier, civilian clothing had been confiscated in Magadan; hundreds of thousands of fur coats from hundreds of convict gangs that had been shipped to the Far north of Misery. These were warm coats, sweaters, and suits that could have served as precious bribes to save a life in some decisive hour. But all roads back were cut off in the Magadan bathhouse. Mountains of civilian clothing rose in the yard. They were higher than the water tower, higher than the bathhouse roof. Mountains of clothing, mountains of tragedies, mountains of human fates suddenly snapped. All who left the bathhouse were doomed to death. How these people had fought to protect their goods from the camp criminal element, from the blatant piracy that raged in the barracks, the cattle cars, the transit points! All that had been saved, hidden from the thieves, was confiscated in the bathhouse by the state.

How simple it all was! Only two years had passed, and now everything was being repeated.

Civilian clothing that had reached the mines was confiscated later. I remember how I had been awakened in the middle of the night. There were searches in the barracks every day, and every day people were led away. I sat on my cot and

smoked. I had no civilian clothing. It had all been left in the
Magadan bathhouse. But some of my comrades had civilian
clothing. These were precious things—symbols of a different
life. They may have been rotting, torn, unmended, because no
one had either the time or the strength to sew. Nevertheless
they were treasured.

Each of us stood at his place and waited. The investigator
sat next to the lamp and wrote up reports on confiscated items.

I sat on the bunk and smoked, neither upset or indignant,
but overwhelmed by one single desire—that the search be
ended as quickly as possible so we could go back to sleep. But
our orderly, whose name was Praga, began to hack away at his
suit with an ax, tore the sheets into shreds, chopped up his
shoes.

"Just rags, all they'll get is rags."

"Take that ax away from him," shouted the inspector.

Praga threw the ax on the floor. The search stopped. The
items Praga had torn and cut were his own things. They had
not yet managed to write up a report on them. When he realized they were not about to seize him, Praga shredded his civilian clothing before our very eyes. And before the eyes of the
investigator.

That had been a year ago. And now it was happening
again.

Everyone was excited, upset, and had difficulty falling
asleep again.

"There's no difference between the criminals who rob us
and the government that robs us," I said. And everyone agreed
with me.

As watchman, Skoroseev started his shift about two hours
before we did. Two abreast—all the taiga path would allow—
we reached the office, angry and offended. Naïve longing for
justice sits deep in man—perhaps even too deep to root out.
After all, why be offended? Angry? Indignant? This damn
search was just one instance of thousands. But at the bottom
of each of our souls something stronger than freedom,

stronger than life's experience, was boiling. The faces of the convicts were dark with rage.

On the office porch stood the camp chief, Victor Nikolae-vich Plutalov. The chief's face was also dark with rage. Our tiny column stopped in front of the office, and Plutalov called me into the office.

"So, you say the state is worse than the camp criminals?" Plutalov stared at me from under lowered brows, biting his lips and sitting uncomfortably on a stool behind his desk.

I said nothing. Skoroseev! The impatient Mr. Plutalov didn't conceal his stoolie, didn't wait for two hours! Or was something else the matter?

"I don't give a damn how you run off at the mouth. But what am I supposed to do if it's reported to me? Or, in your language, someone squeals?"

"Yes sir, it's called squealing."

"All right, get back to work. You'd all eat each other alive if you had the chance. Politicians! A universal language. Everyone is going to understand one another. But I'm in charge here. I have to do something, if they squeal to me. . . ."

Plutalov spat angrily.

A week passed, and I was shipped off with the latest group to leave the blessed prospecting group for the big mine. On the very first day I took the place of a horse in a wooden yoke, heaving with my chest against a wooden log.

Skoroseev remained in the prospecting group.

They were putting on an amateur performance in camp, and the wandering actor, who was also master of ceremonies, came running out to encourage the nervous performers off-stage (one of the hospital wards). "The performance's going great! It's a great performance!" he would whisper into the ear of each participant. "It's a great performance!" he announced loudly and strode back and forth, wiping the sweat from his forehead with a dirty rag.

Everything was very professional; the wandering actor had himself once been a star. Someone on stage was reading aloud a story of Zoschenko, "Lemonade." The master of ceremonies leaned over to me:

"Give me a smoke!"

"Sure."

"You wouldn't believe it," the master of ceremonies said
suddenly, "but if I didn't know better, I'd swear it was that
bitch Skoroseev."

"Skoroseev?" Now I knew whose intonations the voice on
stage had reminded me of.

"I'm an Esperantist. Do you understand? It's a universal
language. No 'basic English' for me. That's what I got my sentence for. I'm a member of the Moscow Society of Esperantists."

"Oh, you mean Article 5, Paragraph 6? A spy?"

"Obviously."

"Ten years?"

"Fifteen."

"But where does Skoroseev fit in?"

"Skoroseev was the vice-chairman of the society. He's the
one who sold us all out, testified against everyone."

"Kind of short?"

"Yeah."

"Where's he now?"

"I don't know, but I'd strangle him with my bare hands. I
ask you as a friend [I had known the actor for about two
hours—no more]: hit him in the face if you meet him. Right in
the mug, and half your sins will be forgiven you."

"Half, for sure?"

"For sure."

But the reader of Zoschenko's "Lemonade" was already
walking offstage. It wasn't Skoroseev, but tall, lanky Baron
Mendel. He looked like a prince from the Romanov dynasty
and counted Pushkin among his ancestors. I was somewhat
disappointed as I looked Pushkin's descendant over, and the
master of ceremonies was already leading his next victim onto
the stage. He declaimed Gorky's "Wind gathers the clouds
over the sea's gray plain."

"Just listen," the baron leaned over to me. "What kind of poetry is that? That kind of howling wind and thunder isn't poetry. Just imagine! In that same year, that same day and hour, Blok wrote his 'Oath in Fire and Gloom,' and Bely wrote 'Gold in Azure'. . . ."

I envied the baron's happiness. He could lose himself, flee into verse.

Many years had passed, and nothing was forgotten. I arrived in Magadan after being released from camp and was attempting to free myself in a true fashion, to cross that terrible sea over which I had once been brought to Kolyma. And although I realized how difficult it would be to exist during my eternal wanderings, I didn't want to remain on the cursed Kolyma soil by choice.

I had little money, and a truck headed in my direction had brought me to Magadan for a ruble per kilometer. The town was shrouded by a white fog. I had acquaintances here. They had to be here. But one seeks out acquaintances here in the day, and not at night. At night, no one will open even for a familiar voice. I needed a roof over my head, a berth, sleep.

I stood in the bus station and gazed at the floor which was completely covered with bodies, objects, sacks, crates. If worse came to worst . . . It was as cold here as on the street, perhaps forty-five degrees below zero. The iron stove had no fire in it, and the station door was constantly opening.

"Don't I know you?"

In the savage frost I was glad to see even Skoroseev. We shook hands through our mittens.

"You can stay at my place. My house is nearby. I was released quite a while back. Got a mortgage and built a house. Even got married." Skoroseev burst out laughing. "We'll have some tea. . . ."

It was so cold, I agreed. For a long time we made our way over the hills and ruts of nighttime Magadan with its shroud of cold milky darkness.

"Yes, I built a house," Skoroseev was saying as I smoked,

resting up. "Got a government loan. Decided to build a nest. A northern nest."

I drank some tea, lay down, and fell asleep. But I slept badly in spite of my distant journey. Somehow yesterday had been lived badly. When I woke up, washed, and had a smoke, I understood how I had lived yesterday badly.

"Well, I'll be going. I have a friend not far from here."

"Leave your suitcase. If you find your friends, you can come back for it."

"No, this is too far away."

"I really wish you'd stay. After all, we are old friends."

"Yes," I said. "Good-bye."

I buttoned my coat, picked up the suitcase and reached for the door handle. "Good-bye."

"What about the money?" said Skoroseev.

"What money?"

"For the night. It's not free."

"I'm sorry. I didn't realize that."

I put down the suitcase, unbuttoned my coat, groped for the money in my pockets and paid. The fog was milky yellow in the day.

The Train

>>

AT THE TRAIN STATION in Irkutsk I lay down in the clear sharp light of an electric bulb. All my money was sewn into a cotton belt that had been made for me in the shop two years earlier; the time had finally come for it to render service. Carefully, stepping over legs, selecting a path among the dirty, stinking, ragged bodies, a policeman patrolled the train station. Better still, there was a military patrol with red arm bands and automatic rifles. There was no way the policeman could have controlled the criminals in the crowd, and this fact had probably been established long before my arrival at the train station. It was not that I was afraid my money would be stolen. I had lost any sense of fear much earlier. It was just that things were easier with money than without.

The light shone directly in my face, but lights had shone in my eyes thousands of times before and I had learned to sleep very well with the light on. I turned up the collar of my pea jacket, shoved my hands into the sleeves of the opposite arms, let my felt boots slip from my feet a little, and fell asleep. I wasn't worried about drafts. Everything was familiar: the screech of the train whistle, the moving cars, the train station, the policeman, the bazaar next to the train station. It was as if I had just awakened from a dream that had lasted for years. And suddenly I was afraid and felt a cold sweat form on my body. I was frightened by the terrible strength of man, his desire and ability to forget. I realized I was ready to forget everything, to cross out twenty years of my life. And what years! And when I understood this, I conquered myself. I knew I would not permit my memory to forget everything that I had seen. And I regained my calm and fell asleep.

I woke, turned my foot rags so that the dry side was facing inward, and washed myself in the snow. Black splashes flew in all directions. Then I set out for town—my first town in eighteen years. Yakutsk was a large village. The Lena River had receded far from the town, but the inhabitants feared its return, its floods, and the sandy field of the riverbed was empty, filled only by a snowstorm. Here in Irkutsk were large buildings, the hustle and bustle of people, stores.

I bought some knit underwear; I hadn't worn that kind of underwear for eighteen years. I experienced an inexpressible bliss at standing in line and paying. The size? I forgot my size. The biggest one. The saleswoman shook her head disapprovingly. Size fifty-five? She wrapped up underwear that I was never to wear, for my size was fifty-one. I learned that in Moscow. All the salesgirls were dressed in identical blue dresses. I bought a shaving brush and a penknife. These wonderful things were ridiculously cheap. In the north everything was homemade—shaving brushes and penknives. I went into a bookstore. In the used-book section they were selling Solovyov's *History of Russia*—850 rubles for the entire set. No, I wouldn't buy books until I got to Moscow. But to hold books, to stand next to the counter of a bookstore was like a dish of hot meaty soup . . . like a glass of the water of life.

In Irkutsk our paths separated. In Yakutsk we walked around town in a group, bought plane tickets together, and stood in lines together—all four of us. It never entered our thoughts to entrust our money to anyone. That was not the custom in our world. I reached the bridge and looked down at the boiling, green Angara River. Its powerful waters were so clean, they were transparent right down to the bottom. Touching the cold brown rail with my frozen hand, I inhaled the gasoline fumes and dust of a city in winter, watched the hurrying pedestrians, and realized how much I was an urban dweller. I realized that the most precious time for man was when he was acquiring a homeland, but when love and family had not yet been born. This was childhood and early youth. Overwhelmed, I greeted Irkutsk with all my heart. Irkutsk was my Moscow.

As I approached the train station, someone tapped me on the shoulder. "Someone wants to talk to you," a tow-headed boy in a quilted jacket said and led me into the darkness. All at once a short man dove out into the light and began to examine my person.

I realized from his look just whom I had to deal with. His gaze, cowardly and impudent, flattering and hating, was familiar to me. Other snouts peered from the darkness. I had no need to know them; they would all appear in their own time— with knives, with nails, with sharpened stakes in their hands. . . . But for now my encounter was limited to one face with pale earthy skin, with swollen eyelids and tiny lips that seemed glued onto a shaven receding chin. "Who are you?" He stretched out his dirty hand with its long fingernails. I had to answer, for neither the policeman nor the patrol could render any help here.

"You're—from Kolyma?"

"Yes, from Kolyma."

"Where did you work there?"

"I was a paramedic in a geological exploration group."

"A paramedic? A doc? You drank the blood of people like us. We have a few things to say to you."

In my pocket I clasped the new penknife that I had just bought and said nothing. Luck was my only hope. Patience and luck are what saved and save us. These are the two whales supporting the convict's world. And luck came to me.

The darkness separated. "I know him." A new figure appeared in the light, one that was totally unfamiliar to me. I have an excellent memory for faces, but I had never seen this man.

"You?" The finger with the long nail described an arc.

"Yes, he worked in Kolyma," the unknown man said. "They say he was a decent sort. Helped people like us. They said good things about him."

The finger with the nail disappeared.

"Okay, clear out," the thief said in an unhappy tone. "We'll think about it."

I was lucky that I didn't have to spend the night at the station. The train was leaving for Moscow in the evening.

In the morning the light from the electric bulbs seemed heavy. The bulbs were murky and didn't want to go out. Through the opening and closing doors could be seen the Irkutsk day—cold and bright. Swarms of people packed the corridors and filled up every square centimeter of space on the cement floor and the dirty benches as soon as anyone moved, stood up, left. There was an endless standing in line before the ticket windows. A ticket to Moscow, a ticket to Moscow, the rest can be worked out later. . . . Not to Jambul, as the travel

orders instructed. But who cared about travel orders in this
heap of humanity, in this constant movement?

My turn at the window finally arrived, and I began to pull
money from my pockets in jerky movements and to push the
packet of gleaming bills through the opening where they
would disappear as inevitably as my life had disappeared until
that moment. But the miracle continued, and the window
threw out some solid object. It was rough, hard, and thin, like a
wafer of happiness—a ticket to Moscow. The cashier shouted
something to the effect that reserved berths were mixed with
nonreserved ones, that a truly reserved car would be available
only tomorrow or the day after tomorrow. I understood nothing
except the words tomorrow and today. Today, today. Clasping
my ticket firmly and attempting to feel all its corners with the
deadened senses of my frostbitten hand, I pulled myself free
and made my way to an open spot. I had just come from the far
north by plane and I had no extra things—just a small plywood suitcase—the same one I had unsuccessfully tried to sell
back in Adygalakh to get the money together to leave for Moscow. My traveling expenses had not been paid, but that was a
meaningless detail. The main thing was this firm cardboard
rectangle of a railroad ticket.

I caught my breath somewhere in a corner of the train
station (my spot under the light was, of course, occupied) and
set out across town, to the departure area.

Boarding had already begun. On a low hill stood a toy
train, unbelievably small—just a few dirty cardboard boxes
placed together among hundreds of other cardboard boxes
where railroad employees lived and hung out their frozen
wash to splash under the blows of the wind.

My train was in no way distinguishable from these
railroad cars that had been transformed into dormitories.

The train didn't look like a train that was about to set out
in a few hours for Moscow. Rather, it looked like a dormitory.
People were coming down the stairs of the cars, moving back
and forth, and carrying things over their heads—just as others

were doing around the dormitories. I realized that the train lacked the most important thing—a locomotive. Neither did any of the dormitories have a locomotive, and my train looked like a dormitory. I wouldn't have believed that these cars could carry me away to Moscow, but boarding was already taking place.

There was a battle, a terrible battle at the entrance to the car. It seemed that work had ended two hours early today and everyone had come running home, to the barracks, to the warm stove, and they were all trying to get in the door.

Inside you could forget about finding a conductor. . . . Each person sought out his own place, dug himself in and maintained his own position. Of course, my reserved middle berth was occupied by some drunken lieutenant who belched endlessly. I dragged the lieutenant down and showed him my ticket. "I have a ticket for this spot too," he explained in a peaceable fashion, hiccuped, slipped down to the floor, and immediately fell asleep.

The car kept filling up with people. Suitcases and enormous bales were lifted up and disappeared somewhere above. There was an acrid smell of sheepskin coats, human sweat, dirt, and carbolic acid.

"A prison car, a prison car," I repeated lying on my back, jammed into the narrow space between the middle and upper berths. The lieutenant, his collar opened and his face red and wrinkled, crawled upward past me. He got a grip on something, pulled himself upward, and disappeared.

In the confusion, amid the shouts of this prison car, I missed the main thing that I needed to hear, that which I had dreamed of for seventeen years, that which had become for me a sort of symbol of the "mainland," a symbol of life. I hadn't given it a thought during the battle for the berth. I hadn't heard the train whistle. But the cars shuddered and began to move and our car, our prison car, set out somewhere just as if I were beginning to fall asleep and the barracks was moving before my very eyes.

I forced myself to realize that I was headed for Moscow.

At some switch point close to Irkutsk the car lurched and the figure of the lieutenant gripping his berth leaned out and hung down. He belched and vomited on my berth and that of my neighbor, who was wearing not a quilted coat or a pea jacket but a real overcoat with a fur collar. The man swore mightily and began to clean off the vomit.

My neighbor had with him an infinite number of plaited wicker baskets, some sewn up with burlap and some without burlap. From time to time women wearing country kerchiefs would appear from the depths of the car with similar wicker baskets on their shoulders. The women would shout something to my neighbor and he would wave back to them in a friendly fashion.

"My sister-in-law! She's going to visit relatives in Tashkent," he explained to me although I had asked for no explanations.

My neighbor was eager to open his nearest basket and show its contents. Aside from a wrinkled suit and a few small items it was empty. But it did contain a number of photographs, family and individual pictures in enormous mats. Some of them were daguerreotypes. The larger photographs were removed from the basket, and my neighbor eagerly explained in detail who was standing where, who was killed in the war, who received a medal, who was studying to be an engineer. "And here I am," he would inevitably say, pointing somewhere in the middle of the photograph, at which juncture everyone to whom he showed the photograph would meekly, politely, and sympathetically nod his head.

On the third day of our life in this rattling car my neighbor, having sized me up in detail, no doubt very correctly despite the fact that I had said nothing of myself, waited until the attention of our other neighbors was distracted and said quickly to me:

"I have to make a transfer in Moscow. Can you help me carry one basket across the scales?"

"I'm being met in Moscow."

"Oh, yes. I forgot you're being met."

"What do you have in the baskets?"

"What? Sunflower seeds. We'll take galoshes back from Moscow. That sort of 'private enterprise' is illegal, of course, but. . . ."

I did not get out at any of the stations. I had food with me, and I was afraid the train would leave without me, would surely leave without me. I was convinced something bad would happen; happiness cannot continue endlessly.

Opposite me on the middle berth lay a man in a fur coat. He was infinitely drunk and had no cap or mittens. His drunken friends had put him on the train and entrusted his ticket to the conductor. The next day he got out at some station, returned with a bottle of some sort of dark wine, drank it all straight from the bottle, and threw the bottle on the floor. The bottle could be turned in for the deposit and the woman conductor agilely caught it and carried it off to her conductor's lair which was filled with blankets that no one in the mixed car rented and sheets that no one needed. Behind the same barrier of blankets in the conductor's compartment a prostitute had set up shop on the upper berth. She was returning from Kolyma, and perhaps she wasn't a prostitute but had simply been transformed into a prostitute by Kolyma. . . . This lady sat not far from me on the lower berth, and the light from the swinging lamp fell on her utterly exhausted face with lips reddened by some substitute for lipstick. People would approach her and then they would disappear with her into the conductors' compartment. "Fifty rubles," said the lieutenant who had sobered up and turned out to be a very pleasant young man.

He and I played a fascinating game. Whenever a new passenger entered the car, he and I would try to guess the new arrival's age and profession. We would exchange observations and he would strike up a conversation with the passenger and come back to me with the answer.

Thus the lady who had painted lips but whose nails lacked any trace of polish was determined by us to be a member of the medical profession. The obviously fake leopard coat she wore testified that its wearer was probably a nurse or orderly, but not a doctor. A doctor wouldn't have worn an artificial fur coat. Back then nylon and synthetic fabrics were unheard of. Our conclusion turned out to be correct.

From time to time a two-year-old child, dirty, ragged, and blue-eyed, would run past our compartment from somewhere in the depths of the railroad car. His pale cheeks were covered with scabs of some kind. In a minute or two the young father, who had heavy, strong working hands, would come after him with firm confident strides. He would catch the boy, and the child would laugh and smile at his father who would smile back at him and return him to his place in joyous bliss. I learned their story, a common story in Kolyma. The father had just served a criminal sentence and was returning to the mainland. The child's mother chose not to return, and the father was taking his son with him, having firmly resolved to tear the child (and perhaps himself) free from the vise-like clutches of Kolyma. Why didn't the mother leave? Perhaps it was the usual story: she'd found another man, liked the free life of Kolyma, and didn't want to be in the situation of a second-rate citizen on the mainland. . . . Or perhaps her youth had faded? Or maybe her love, her Kolyma love, had ended? Who knows? The mother had served a sentence under Article 58 of the Criminal Code, an article classifying political prisoners. Thus her crime had been of the most common and everyday sort. She knew what a return to the mainland would mean—a new sentence, new torments. There were no guarantees against a new sentence in Kolyma either, but at least she wouldn't be hunted as all were hunted over there.

I neither learned nor wanted to learn anything. The nobility, the goodness, the love for his child was all I saw in this father who himself must previously have seen very little of his son. The boy had been in a nursery.

His clumsy hands unbuttoned the child's pants with their enormous unmatched buttons sewn on by rough, inept, but good hands. Both the boy and the father exuded happiness. The two-year-old child didn't know the word "mama." He shouted, "Papa, papa!" He and this dark-skinned mechanic played with each other among the throng of card sharks and wheeler-dealers with their bales and baskets. These two people were, of course, happy.

But there was no more sleep for the passenger who had slept for two days from the moment we had left Irkutsk and who had awakened only to drink another bottle of vodka or cognac or whatever it was. The train lurched. The sleeping passenger crashed to the floor and groaned—over and over again. The conductors sent for an ambulance and it was discovered that he had a broken shoulder. He was carried away on a stretcher, and disappeared from my life.

Suddenly there appeared in the car the figure of my savior. Perhaps "savior" is too lofty a word since, after all, nothing important or bloody had occurred. My acquaintance sat, not recognizing me and as if not wanting to recognize me. Nevertheless we exchanged glances and I approached him. "I just want to go home and see my family." These were the last words I heard from this criminal.

And that is all: the glaring light of the bulb at the Irkutsk train station, the "businessman" hauling around random pictures for camouflage, vomit avalanching down onto my berth from the throat of the young lieutenant, the sad prostitute on the upper berth in the conductors' compartment, the dirty two-year-old boy blissfully shouting "Papa! Papa!" This is all I remember as my first happiness, the unending happiness of "freedom." The roar of Moscow's Yaroslav Train Station met me like an urban surf; I had arrived at the city I loved above all other cities on earth. The train came to a halt and I could see the dear face of my wife who met me just as she had met me so many times before after each of my numerous trips. This trip, however, had been a long one—almost seventeen years.

Most important, I was not returning from a business trip. I was returning from hell.

The Used-Book Dealer

>>

IT ALL BEGAN some time before my release from Kolyma. I had been transferred from night into day—clearly a promotion, a confirmation, a success along the dangerous path to salvation of an orderly recruited from among the patients. I never noticed who took my place, for in those days I lacked the strength necessary for curiosity and I hoarded my movements—spiritual and physical. I'd accomplished resurrections before, and I knew how dearly one paid for unnecessary curiosity.

In a nocturnal half-sleep and out of the corner of my eye, however, I saw a pale dirty face grown over with reddish bristles, cavernous eyes—eyes whose color I couldn't remember—and hooked frostbitten fingers clutching the handle of the smoky kettle. The barracks' hospital night was so dark and thick that the flame of the kerosene lantern, wavering and flickering as if in the wind, was not enough to light up the corridor, the ceiling, the wall, the door, the floor. The light ripped from the darkness only a piece of the night: a corner of the bedside table and the pale face bent over it. The new man on duty was dressed in the same gown that I used to wear. It was a dirty, torn gown—an ordinary gown intended for the patients. During the day this filthy garment hung in the hospital ward and at night was donned over the quilted jacket of the orderly on duty, who was always chosen from among the patients. The flannel was so extraordinarily thin it was transparent, but nevertheless it didn't tear. Perhaps the patients made

no abrupt movements for fear that the gown would disintegrate. Or perhaps they were unable to.

The semicircle of light swayed back and forth, wavered,
reached out in sudden movements. It seemed that the cold
and not the wind swung the light above the night table of the
orderly on duty. It was not the wind, but the cold itself that
moved the light. Within the circle of light swung a face
twisted with hunger, and hooked fingers searched the kettle's
bottom for something no spoon could catch. Even frostbitten,
the fingers were more reliable than a spoon; at once I understood the essence of the movement, the language of gesture.

There was no reason for me to know all this; I was only
the day orderly.

But a few days later, fate was unexpectedly prodded by a
sudden and hurried departure in the back of a jolting truck.
The vehicle crawled south toward Magadan along the bed of a
nameless river that served as a winter road through the taiga.
In the back of the truck two human beings were repeatedly
tossed upward and dropped back onto the floor with a wooden
thud as if they were logs. The guard was sitting in the cab, and
I couldn't tell if I was being struck by a piece of wood or a man.
At one of the feeding stops my neighbor's greedy chomping
struck me as familiar, and I recognized the hooked fingers and
the pale dirty face.

We didn't speak to each other; each feared he might
frighten off his happiness, his convict joy. The truck hurried
on into the next day, and the road came to an end.

We had both been selected by the camp to take paramedic
courses. Magadan, the hospital, and the courses were cloaked
in fog, a white Kolyma fog. Were there markers, road markers? Would they accept political prisoners convicted under
Article 58 of the Criminal Code? Only those who came under
Point 10. And how about my neighbor in the rear of the truck?
He too was ASA—anti-Soviet agitation. That was considered
the same as Point 10.

There was an examination on the Russian language. A

dictation. The grades were posted the same day. I got an "A."
After that came a written examination on mathematics, and I
received another "A." It was taken for granted that future
students were not required to know the fine points of the Soviet Constitution. . . . I lay on the bunk, dirty and still literally
lousy. The job of orderly didn't destroy lice. But perhaps it only
seemed that way to me; lice infestation is one of the camp
neuroses. I didn't have lice any more, but I still couldn't force
myself to get used to the thought or, rather, to the feeling that
the lice were gone. I had experienced that feeling two or three
times. As for the "constitution" or political economics, such
things were no more intended for us than was the luxurious
Astoria Hotel. In Butyr Prison the guard on duty in our cell
block shouted at me: "Why do you keep asking about the constitution? Your constitution is the Criminal Code!" And he was
right. Yes, the Criminal Code was our constitution. That was a
long time ago. A thousand years. The fourth subject was
chemistry. My grade was "C."

Oh, how those convict students strove for knowledge
when the stakes of the game were life! How former professors
of medicine strove to beat their lifesaving knowledge into the
heads of ignoramuses and idiots. From the storekeeper Silai-
kin down to the Tartar writer Min-Shabay, none of them had
ever shown the slightest interest in medicine.

Twisting his thin lips in a sneer, the surgeon asked:

"Who invented penicillin?"

"Fleming!" The answer was given not by me, but by my
neighbor from the district hospital. His red bristles were
shaven off, and there remained only an unhealthy pale puffi-
ness in the cheeks. (He had gorged himself on soup, I immediately realized.)

I was amazed at the red-headed student's knowledge. The
surgeon sized up the triumphant "Fleming." Who are you,
night orderly? Who? Who were you before prison?

"I'm a captain. A captain of the engineering troops. At the
beginning of the war I was chief of the fortified area on Dicson

Island. We had to put up fortifications in a hurry. In the fall of
'41 when the morning fog broke we saw the German raider
Graf Spee in the bay. The raider shot up all our fortifications
point-blank. And left. And I got ten years. 'If you don't believe
it, consider it a fairy tale.' "

All the students studied through the night, passionately
soaking up knowledge with all the appetite of men condemned
to death but suddenly given the chance of a reprieve.

After a meeting with the higher-ups, however, Fleming's
spirits lifted and he brought a novel to the barracks, where everyone else was studying. As he finished off some boiled fish,
the remnants of someone else's feast, he carelessly leafed
through the book.

Catching my ironic smile, Fleming said:

"What's the difference? We've been studying for three
months now, and anyone who's lasted this long will finish and
get his certificate. Why should I go crazy studying? You have
to know how to look at things."

"No," I said. "I want to learn to treat people. I want to
learn a real skill."

"Knowing how to live is a real skill."

It was then that I learned that Fleming's claim to having
been a captain was only a mask, another mask on that pale
prison face. The rank of captain was real; the bit about the engineering troops was an invention. Fleming had been in the
NKVD—the secret police—with the rank of captain. Information on his past had been accumulating drop by drop for several years. A drop was a measure of time, something like a
water clock. This drop fell on the bare skull of a person being
interrogated; such was the water clock of the Leningrad
prisons of the thirties. Sand clocks measured the time allotted
for exercise. Water clocks measured the time of confession,
the period of investigation. Clocks of sand drained with fleet-
ing speed; water clocks were tormentingly slow. Water clocks
didn't count or measure minutes; they measured the human
soul, the will, destroying it drop by drop, eroding it just as

water erodes a rock. This piece of folklore about investigations was very popular in the thirties and even in the twenties.

Captain Fleming's words were gathered drop by drop, and the treasure turned out to be priceless. Fleming himself considered it priceless. It could not have been otherwise, and I remember our conversations very clearly.

"Do you know the greatest secret of our time?"

"What?"

"The trials of the thirties. You know how they prepared them? I was in Leningrad at the time. I worked with Zakovsky. The preparation of the trials was all chemistry, medicine, pharmacology. They had more will suppressants than you could shake a stick at. You don't think that if such suppressants exist, they wouldn't use them? The Geneva Agreement or something like that . . .

"It would have been too human to possess chemical will suppressants and not use them on the 'internal front.' This and only this is the secret of the trials of the thirties, the open trials, open to foreign correspondents and to any Feuchtwanger. There were no 'doubles' in those trials. The secret of the trials was the secret of pharmacology. . . ."

I lay on the short uncomfortable bunk in the empty student barracks which was shot through with rays of sunshine and listened to these admissions.

"There were experiments earlier—in the sabotage trials, for example. That comic trial of Ramzin touches on pharmacology very slightly."

Fleming's story seeped through drop by drop, or was it his own blood that fell on my bare memory? What sort of drops were these—blood, tears, or ink? They weren't ink, and they weren't tears.

"Of course, there are instances when medicine is powerless. Or sometimes the solutions aren't prepared properly. There were rules to double-check everything."

"Where are those doctors now?"

"Who knows? On the moon probably . . ."

The investigator has all the latest scientific discoveries and technology in his arsenal, the latest in pharmacology.

"It wasn't cabinet 'A'—toxic or poisonous—and not cabinet 'B'—strong effect. . . ." It turns out that the Latin word "hero" is translated in Russian as "having a strong effect." And where were Captain Fleming's medications kept? In cabinet "C," the crime cabinet or in cabinet "M"—for magic?

A person who had access to cabinet "C," cabinet "M," and the most advanced scientific discoveries had to take a course for hospital orderlies to learn that man has one liver, that the liver is not a paired organ. He learned about blood circulation three hundred years after Harvey.

The secret was kept in laboratories, in underground offices, in stinking cages where the animals smelled like convicts in the Magadan transit prison in '38. In comparison with this transit prison, Butyr was a model of surgical immaculateness and smelled more like an operating room than an animal's cage.

All scientific and technological discoveries are checked first of all for any military significance, even to the extent of speculating on their possible future military uses. And only that which has been sifted through by the generals and found to have no relevance to war is given over for the common use.

Medicine, chemistry, pharmacology have long since been placed under military control. Throughout the world, institutes for the study of the brain have always accumulated the results of experiments, observations. Borgia's poisons were always a weapon of *Realpolitik*. The twentieth century brought with it an extraordinary tide of pharmacological and chemical preparations for the control of the psyche.

But if it is possible to obliterate fear with medicine, the opposite is true a thousand times—it is possible to suppress the human will by injections, by pure pharmacology and chemistry without making use of any "physical" methods such as breaking ribs and knocking out teeth, stubbing out cigarettes on the body of the person under investigation, or trampling him with the heels of boots.

These two schools of investigation were known as physics and chemistry. The physicists regarded purely physical persuasion as the cornerstone of their building and viewed beatings as a means of revealing the moral foundations of the world. Once revealed, how base and worthless were the depths of human essence! Beatings could achieve any testimony. Under the threat of a club, inventors made scientific discoveries, wrote verse and novels. The fear of beating and the stomach's scale for measuring its "ration" worked miracles.

Beating is a sufficiently weighty and effective psychological weapon.

Many useful results were produced by the famous and ubiquitous "conveyor" in which the investigators alternated without giving the arrested person a chance to sleep. After seventeen days without sleep a man loses his sanity. Has this scientific observation been made in the offices of political investigators?

But neither did the chemical school retreat.

Physics could guarantee material for "Special Councils" and all sorts of "troikas" where a triumvirate of judges would make their decisions behind closed doors. The School of Physical Inducement, however, could not be applied in open trials. The School of Physical Inducement (I believe that's the term used by Stanislavsky) could not publicly present its theater of blood, could not have prepared the "open trials" that made all mankind tremble. The preparation of such spectacles was within the realm of competency of the chemists.

Twenty years after these conversations with Fleming I include in this story lines taken from a newspaper article:

"Through the application of certain psychopharmacological agents it is possible, for example, to remove a human being's sense of fear for a limited time. Of particular importance is the fact that the clarity of his consciousness is not in the least disturbed in the process.

"Later even more unexpected facts come to light. Persons whose 'B phases' of dream were suppressed for a long period of time—in the given instance for seventeen nights in a row—began to experience various disturbances in their psychic condition and conduct."

What is this? Fragments of testimony of some former NKVD officer during the trial of the judges? A letter from Vyshinsky or Riumin before their deaths? No, these are paragraphs taken from a scientific article written by a member of the Soviet Academy of Sciences. But all this—and a hundred times more—was learned, tried, and applied in the thirties in the preparation of the "open trials"!

Pharmacology was not the only weapon in the investigator's aresenal of those years. Fleming mentioned a name that I knew well.

Ornaldo!

Of course! Ornaldo was a famous hypnotist who appeared frequently in the twenties in Moscow circuses, and not only in Moscow.

Oranaldo's speciality was mass hypnosis. Books on hypnosis are illustrated with photographs of his famous tours. "Oranaldo," of course, was a pseudonym. His real name was M. A. Smirnov, and he was a Moscow doctor. There were posters pasted all the way around special drums used for theatrical advertisements. Paolo-Svishev had a photograph hanging in the window on Stoleshnikov Lane. It was an enormous photograph of human eyes with the inscription "The Eyes of Ornaldo." Even now I remember those eyes and the emotional confusion that I experienced whenever I heard or saw Ornaldo's circus act. There are photographs of Ornaldo's performances taken in 1929 in Baku. Then he left the stage.

"Beginning in the middle of the thirties Ornaldo was in the secret employment of the NKVD."

The shiver of a revealed secret ran down my back.

Fleming would frequently, and for no special reason, praise Leningrad. Perhaps it would be more correct to say that he admitted he wasn't a native Leningrader. In fact, he had been recruited from the provinces by the aesthetes of the NKVD in the twenties as their worthy replacement. They grafted onto him tastes much broader than those provided by an ordinary school education. Not just Turgenev and Nekrasev, but Balmont and Sologub, not just Pushkin, but Gumilyov as well:

" 'And you, watchdogs of the king, pirates guarding gold in the dark port . . .' I'm not quoting the line incorrectly, am I?"

"No, that's right."

"I can't remember the rest. Am I a watchdog of the king? Of the state?"

And smiling—both to himself and his past—he told with reverence how he had touched the file of the executed poet Gumilyov, calling it the affar of lycée pupils. It was as if a Pushkinist were telling how he had held the goose quill pen with which Pushkin wrote *Poltava*. It was just as if he had touched the Stone of Kaaba, such was the bliss, the purification in every feature of his face. I couldn't help but think that this too was a way of being introduced to poetry, an amazing, extremely rare manner of introduction in the office of the criminal investigator. Of course the moral values of poetry are not transmitted in the process.

"When reading books I would first of all turn to the notes, the comments. Man is a creature of notes and comments."

"How about the text?"

"Not always. There is always time for that."

Obscene as this may sound, Fleming and his co-workers could partake of culture only in their work as investigators. Their familiarity with persons of literary and social circles was distorted but nevertheless real and genuine in a sense, not concealed behind a thousand masks.

The chief informer on the artistic intelligentsia of those years was Major General Ignatiev. To hear the name of this former czarist diplomat and well-known memoirist was surprising only at first. A steady, thoughtful, and qualified author of all sorts of "memoranda" and surveys of writers' lives, he had served fifty years in the ranks. Forty of those years were spent in the Soviet spy network.

"I'd already read the book *Fifty Years in the Ranks,* and was familiar with his surveys when they introduced me to him. Or him to me," Fleming said thoughtfully. "Not a bad book, *Fifty Years in the Ranks.*"

Fleming didn't care much for newspapers, news, or radio programs. International events scarcely interested him. His emotional life was dominated by a deep resentment for that dark power that had promised the high school boy he would fathom boundless depths, that had carried him to such heights and that had now shamelessly cast him into the abyss.

Fleming's introduction to culture was peculiar—some brief courses and some excursions to the Hermitage. The boy grew into an investigator-aesthete who was shocked by the crude force that was rushing into the "organs of justice" in the thirties. His type was swept away and destroyed by the "new wave" that placed its faith in crude force and despised not only psychological refinements, but even the "conveyor" and the method of not allowing the prisoner to sit down until he confessed. The new wave simply had no patience for any scientific calculations or lofty psychology. It was easier to get results with simple beatings. The slow aesthetes ended up on the moon. It was sheer chance that Fleming remained alive. The new wave couldn't wait.

The hungry gleam in Fleming's eyes faded, and the professional observer again made his voice heard.

"You know, I was watching you during the preoperative conference. You had something on your mind."

"I just want to remember everything, remember it and describe it."

Some images swayed in Fleming's already relaxed and calmed brain.

In the Magadan psychological ward where Fleming had worked there was an enormous Latvian. Everytime the giant sat down to eat, Fleming would sit opposite him, unable to restrain his ecstasy at the sight of such a mountain of food.

Fleming never parted with his pot, the same pot which he had brought from the north. It was a talisman, a Kolyma talisman.

The criminal element in the psychological ward caught a cat, killed it, and cooked it, and gave Fleming a portion as the traditional Kolyma tribe since he was the orderly on duty. Fleming ate the meat and kept silent about the cat. The cat was a pet in the surgical ward.

The students were afraid of Fleming. But whom didn't the students fear? In the hospital Fleming was already working as an orderly, a staff medic. Everyone feared and hated him, sensing in him not only an employee of the secret police but also the master of some unusually important, terrible secret.

The antipathy grew, and the plot thickened after Fleming made a sudden trip to meet with a young Spanish woman. She was a real Spaniard, the daughter of one of the members of the government of the Republic of Spain. She'd been a spy, got involved in a web of provocations, was sentenced and sent to Kolyma to die. It turned out, however, that Fleming was not forgotten by his old and distant friends, his former colleagues. He had to learn something from the woman, to confirm something. But the patient couldn't wait. She had recovered and was being sent to a women's mine. Interrupting his work in the hospital, Fleming suddenly traveled to the mine to meet the woman. He spent two days on the seven-hundred-kilometer road with its incessant flow of vehicles and a checkpoint every kilometer. Fleming was lucky, and he returned from the meeting safe and sound. The event could have taken place in a novel, a feat of camp love. Alas, Fleming didn't travel or accomplish any feats for the sake of love. His was a passion much stronger than love, the highest passion of all, and it would carry Fleming safely past all the camp checkpoints.

Fleming frequently recalled the thirties and the sudden flood of murders and suicides. There was the death of the family of Savinkov, the former revolutionary and terrorist. The son was shot, and the family—the wife, two children, and the wife's mother—did not wish to leave Leningrad. All wrote letters and left them for each other before killing themselves, and Fleming's memory preserved lines of a note from one of the children: "Grandma, we're going to die soon. . . ."

The sentence Fleming had received in connection with the "NKVD Affair" ended in 1950, but he didn't return to Leningrad. He didn't receive permission. His wife, who had retained their room all those years, came to Magadan from Leningrad, wasn't able to make any living arrangements, and went back. Fleming returned to Leningrad just before the Twentieth Party Congress, to the same room he'd lived in before his disaster.

He had to do a lot of running around to get his pension of 1,400 old-style rubles that he was due for his years of service. His camp medical courses notwithstanding, he was not allowed to return to his old "speciality" as an expert on pharmacology. It turned out that all the "former employees," all the veterans of these affairs, all the aesthetes who were still alive, had long since been put out to pasture—all of them, right down to the last courier.

Fleming got a job as a book selector in a secondhand bookstore on Liteiny Prospect. Although his relationship and contact with the Russian intelligentsia was such a peculiar one, he considered himself to be of their bone and flesh. To the end he refused to separate his fate from that of the Russian intelligentsia, feeling, perhaps, that only contact with books could help him preserve his skills, if only he could succeed in living till better times.

In the nineteenth century a captain in the "engineering troops" would have taken vows and retreated to a monastery, as did the Russian writer Konstantin Leontiev. But the dangerous and lofty world of books was tinted with fanaticism for Fleming, and like any other infatuation with books, it served the function of a moral purge. The former admirer of Gumilyov and expert on both Gumilyov's fate and his comments on verse could not become a night watchman. Perhaps use his new profession of hospital orderly? No, better to be a used-book dealer.

"I'm constantly running around, filling out forms. Bring us some rum," Fleming said, turning to the waitress.

"I don't drink," I replied.

"How unfortunate, how inconvenient it is that you don't drink. Katya, he doesn't drink! You understand? I'm constantly working at it. I'll return to my old job."

"If you go back," Katya said with her blue lips, "I'll hang myself or drown myself the very next day!"

"I'm just kidding. I'm always kidding. . . . I'm constantly presenting applications, running around the courts, traveling to Moscow. After all, they took me back in the party. But you know how?"

A wad of rumpled paper emerged from Fleming's jacket pocket.

"Read this. This is Drabkina's testimony. She was a prisoner in my camp in Igarka. Later she published her memoirs under the title *Black Toast*."

Quickly I read through the woman's extensive testimony:

"As head of the camp he treated the prisoners well and for this reason was soon arrested and convicted. . . ."

I leafed through the dirty, sticky testimony of Drabkina which had passed through the careless fingers of government officials.

Bending down to my ear, his breath reeking of rum, Fleming explained hoarsely that he had been a "human being" in camp, even Drabkina confirmed that.

"Do you really need all this?"

"I need it. It fills my life. Who knows, maybe I'll pull it off. How about a drink?"

"I don't drink."

"For years of service. But that's not what I need. . . ."

"Stop it, or I'll hang myself!" Katya shouted.

"She's got a heart condition," Fleming explained.

"Take yourself in hand. Write. You have a good style. I know that from your letters. And a story or a novel is, after all, a confidential letter."

"No, I'm not a writer. I'm going to keep on working at what I started. . . ."

And slobbering in my ear, he whispered something I could make neither head nor tail of, that supposedly there never was any Kolyma and that he himself had spent seventeen days on the "conveyor" in '37 and that his mind was not what it used to be.

"They're publishing a lot of memoirs now. For example, they just published Yakubovich's *In the World of Outcasts*, his memoirs about his years in a czarist penal farm. Let them publish that stuff."

"Have you written any memoirs?"

"No, but there is a book I want to recommend for publication. You know which one? I went to the Lenin Publishing House, but they told me to mind my own business. . . ."

"What book?"

"The notes of Sanson, the Paris executioner. Now those are memoirs!"

"The Parisian executioner?"

"Yes. Sanson guillotined Charlotte Corday and slapped her cheeks, and the cheeks of the severed head blushed. One other thing: they used to give parties that they called 'The Victims' Ball.' Do we have that kind of ball?"

"The Victims' Ball had nothing to do with the Thermidore Period; it was part of the Post-Thermidore Period. Sanson's notes are a forgery."

"What's the difference if they're a forgery or not? Either there was such a book or there wasn't. Let's have some rum. I've tried a lot of drinks in my time, but there's nothing like rum. Rum. Jamaican rum."

Fleming's wife prepared dinner—mountains of greasy food that was almost instantly devoured by the voracious Fleming. An insatiable gluttony remained forever a part of Fleming, just as thousands of other former convicts retained their psychic traumas for the rest of their lives.

The conversation somehow broke off in the early city twilight. I could hear next to me the familiar Kolyma chomping and slurping. I thought of life's strength—hidden in a healthy stomach and bowels that were capable of digesting large quantities. That had been Fleming's defensive reflex against Kolyma—an omnivorous greed. A lack of spiritual fastidiousness acquired behind the desk of a political investigator had also served to prepare him and cushion the shock of his Kolyma fall. As he fell, he perceived no abyss, for he had known all this even earlier and the knowledge saved him by weakening his moral torments, if such torments had even existed. Fleming experienced no additional spiritual traumas; he witnessed the worst and indifferently watched those next to him perish. Prepared to struggle only for his own life, he saved that life, but in his soul there remained a dark footprint that had to be obliterated, purged with penitence. His penitence was a slip of the tongue, a half-hint, a conversation aloud with himself—without regret or condemnation. "The cards just didn't fall my way." Nevertheless Fleming's story was an act of penitence.

"You see this?" he asked me.

"Your party membership card?"

"Right. It's brand new! But it wasn't simple, not at all simple. Six months ago the District Party Committee examined the question of taking me back into the party. They all sat around, read the materials. The secretary of the committee, a Chuvash, announced the decision in a flat way, almost rudely:

" 'Well, it's a clear situation. Write up a resolution: reinstatement with an interruption in membership.'

"It was as if they threw hot coals on me: 'with an interruption in membership.' My first thought was that if I didn't immediately declare I was in disagreement with the resolution, they'd always ask afterward why I was silent when my case was being examined. I mean, that's why you're called in, so you can speak your piece in time, tell them. . . . I raised my hand.

" 'Whad'ya want?' That same rudeness.

"I said: 'I disagree with the resolution. I won't be able to get a job anywhere without being asked to explain the interruption.'

" 'You're a quick one,' the first secretary of the Party District Committee said. 'You're so pushy because you're not hurting for money. How much is your pension?'

"He was right, but I interrupted him and said that I asked for total reinstatement with no interruption in membership.

"And he said: 'Why are you pushing and getting all worked up? You're in blood up to your elbows!'

"There was a roaring in my head. 'How about you,' I said. 'Aren't your hands in blood?'

"The first secretary said: 'This meeting is cancelled.'

" 'And back then, in '37,' I said, 'didn't you bloody your hands then?'

"The first secretary said: 'Enough of this running off at the mouth. We can vote again. Get out of here.'

"I went out into the corridor and they brought me the resolution: 'reinstatement in the party denied.'

"I ran around Moscow like a crazy man, filling out forms, writing letters. The resolution was cancelled. But the original formulation stayed: 'reinstatement with interruption of membership.'

"The person who reported my situation at the Party Control Commission said I should have kept my mouth shut at the District Committee Meeting. I'm still working at it, filling out forms, going to Moscow, filing legal suits. Have a drink."

"I don't drink," I replied.

"This isn't rum, it's cognac. Five-star cognac! For you."

"Take the bottle away."

"I'll do just that, carry it away, take it with me. You won't be offended?"

"Not in the least."

A year after this Leningrad supper I received a last letter from the used-book dealer: "My wife died suddenly while I was away from Leningrad. I arrived six months later and saw her grave and a snapshot of her in the coffin. Don't condemn me for my weakness; I have all my wits about me, but I can't get anything done. I live as if in a dream and have lost all interest in life. I know this will pass, but I need time. What did she see in her life? Dragged herself from one prison to another with packages and legal certificates. Social contempt, the trip to be with me in Magadan, a life of poverty, and now this—the end. Forgive me, I'll write more later. Yes, I'm in good health, but is the society I live in healthy? All the best."